God, how she wanted to be comforted.

To be touched like Eric was touching her now. She wanted to be the one taking the attention and affection instead of constantly having to give more and more of herself.

"Sofia," he said again, his voice sending low flutters through her belly.

Really, no matter what the question was, the answer was simple. "Yes."

His hands slid to a stop on the curve of her calves. Funny how she'd never really thought of calves as being particularly sensual until now. "Will you lie down and rest for a bit?"

She looked at him then. One of the most powerful men in Chicago—and quite possibly the country, to say nothing of the world—was on his knees before her, waiting for her answer.

She uncurled her fingers from where she'd fisted the bedclothes and reached out to stroke his cheek.

"Only if you join me."

* * *

Twins for the Billionaire is part of Harlequin Desire's #1 bestselling series, Billionaires and Babies: Powerful men...wrapped around their babies' little fingers.

Dear Reader,

Can old friends become new lovers? That's the question Eric Jenner finds himself asking when his childhood friend Sofia Bingham comes back into his life. Sofia is a newly widowed mom of twin toddlers and is desperate for something to go right. She applies for the job of office manager at Eric's real estate development empire because she hopes he remembers the way they played together as kids and gives her a chance.

But she doesn't expect Eric to be quite so grown up! And Eric is stunned to see the maid's daughter is now a gorgeous woman in her own right. Although he has strict rules about relationships with his staff, he hires Sofia because she needs the paycheck to take care of her kids. But when Eric offers her much more than friendship, can she put herself first?

Twins for the Billionaire is a sensual story about falling in love and second chances. I hope you enjoy reading this book as much as I enjoyed writing it! Be sure to stop by sarahmanderson.com and sign up for my newsletter at eepurl.com/nv39b to join me as I say, "Long live cowboys!"

Sarah

SARAH M. ANDERSON

TWINS FOR THE BILLIONAIRE

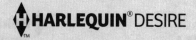

HARLEQUIN® DESIRE

Recycling programs
for this product may
not exist in your area.

ISBN-13: 978-0-373-83879-0

Twins for the Billionaire

Printed in U.S.A.

Sarah M. Anderson may live east of the Mississippi River, but her heart lies out west on the Great Plains. Sarah's book *A Man of Privilege* won an *RT Book Reviews* 2012 Reviewers' Choice Best Book Award. *The Nanny Plan* was a 2016 RITA® Award winner for Contemporary Romance: Short.

Sarah spends her days having conversations with imaginary cowboys and billionaires. Find out more about Sarah's heroes at sarahmanderson.com and sign up for the new-release newsletter at eepurl.com/nv39b.

Books by Sarah M. Anderson

Harlequin Desire

The Bolton Brothers

Straddling the Line
Bringing Home the Bachelor
Expecting a Bolton Baby

The Beaumont Heirs

Not the Boss's Baby
Tempted by a Cowboy
A Beaumont Christmas
His Son, Her Secret
Falling for Her Fake Fiancé
His Illegitimate Heir
Rich Rancher for Christmas

Little Secrets

Little Secrets: Claiming His Pregnant Bride

Billionaire and Babies

Twins for the Billionaire

Visit her Author Profile page at Harlequin.com, or sarahmanderson.com, for more titles.

To the real Adelina and Eduardo—
thanks for all your years of friendship
and support with my family!

Prologue

"So that's it?" Eric Jenner stared at the private investigator's report in his hand. The baby wasn't his. Somehow, he'd known this would be the answer.

Funny how it still hurt like hell.

"That's it." The investigator stood. "Unless there was something else you needed?"

Eric almost laughed. What did he need? He needed a happy ending to this whole mess. But it was clear he wasn't going to get one. Not today. Maybe not ever.

He gritted his teeth. Bad enough that he'd been stood up at the altar—literally. Six months later, the press was still having a field day with the photos of Eric looking stunned next to the priest. In front of six hundred wedding guests. In the Holy Name Cathedral.

But this? He knew he couldn't keep it quiet forever. Prudence had married less than two weeks after she'd left Eric at the altar. Apparently, it was true love. How else to explain Prudence running away with an accountant from her father's company? Who'd fathered Prudence's son and was, according to the PI's account, making her the happiest woman in the world.

Eric was thrilled for them. Really.

He breathed in slowly and exhaled even slower. "If I think of anything else, I'll let you know," he said to the investigator. The man nodded and left.

Eric read the report again. Oddly, he didn't miss Prudence. He didn't lie awake in bed at night, missing her touch. He didn't regret putting the condo he'd bought for her back on the market.

He'd clearly dodged a bullet. Except for one small detail.

That detail had been born at seven pounds, six ounces. He stared at the picture the investigator had included. The baby was bundled up in Prudence's arms, his eyes closed and a little smile on his face. She'd named him Aaron.

Something tightened in Eric's chest. No, Eric didn't miss Prudence at all. But...

Everywhere he went, people had babies. Suddenly, he couldn't avoid them. Even his oldest friend,

Marcus Warren, had recently adopted a baby boy. After he'd married his assistant, of all people.

Eric and Marcus had always competed with each other—who had made the first million (Eric), the first billion (Marcus), who had the finest cars (it changed all the time) or the biggest boat. Eric always won that one, hands down.

It wasn't like the contest was over. But the rules had changed and Eric wasn't ready for this new game. He wasn't ready to stand by as his best friend cooed over his son while his wife looked at them both with love in her eyes.

It should have been nauseating.

Eric and Marcus's entire friendship was built on one-upmanship. But a loving wife and an adorable child?

And now this news from Prudence was the final blow.

One thing was clear. Eric had never lost this badly. To hell with this.

He was Eric Jenner. He owned a quarter of the Chicago skyline, some of the most expensive properties in the world. He'd officially joined the exclusive ranks of billionaires. He was, he had been told, good-looking and good in bed. There wasn't anything he couldn't buy.

What he needed now was distraction. The kind he'd find in the arms of someone new who'd drive thoughts of happy families far from his mind. He hadn't lost anything. He was glad Prudence was gone—that marriage would have been a disaster. He'd gotten lucky. He wasn't tied down. He could do whatever he wanted—and what he wanted was *everything*.

The world was his for the taking. All he had to do was snap his fingers and whatever he wanted was his.

Abruptly, he slammed the report shut and jammed it in the bottom drawer of his desk.

Well.

Almost anything.

It turned out there were some things money couldn't buy.

One

Ten months later...

The elevator door dinged. Sofia Bingham waited for the rest of the crowd to exit first, nerves swirling in her stomach. She was really doing this—interviewing for the job of office manager at Jenner Properties.

Her breath caught in her throat as she stepped into the foyer of Eric Jenner's real estate empire. In her mind, this office had looked exactly the same as Eric's father's real estate office. Jenner and Associates had been a regal office located on the ground floor of a four-story building. John and Elise Jenner had run their exclusive agency on the Gold Coast of Chicago, catering to the rich and the ultrarich.

Her father, Emilio, had started as a janitor before moving up to staging houses for the Jenners and then starting his own company as a bilingual real estate agent. Sofia's mother, Rosa, had been the Jenners' housekeeper and Elise Jenner had had a soft spot for Sofia. Elise had showered Sofia with dresses and toys.

When Sofia had been growing up, the Jenners had seemed like the richest people in the world.

None of that had prepared her for *this*.

Jenner Properties took up the whole of the fortieth floor of the skyscraper at 310 South Wacker Drive. She could see Lake Michigan from here, the sun glittering off the water like a mirage come to life.

She smiled. It had been years since she had seen Eric Jenner, but she wasn't surprised he had a good view of the lake. He'd always loved the water. Not only had he taught her to swim in his family's pool but he'd even taught her how to sail his toy sailboats so they could race.

Around her, more elevators opened and more people poured out. Jenner and Associates had been run primarily by John and Elise Jenner and two other agents. But Jenner Properties was staffed by a small army of very serious-looking people, all of whom wore good suits and better shoes. Sofia looked down at her skirt and jacket combo, the nicest outfit she owned that didn't have baby food stains on it. It was cute—a black-and-white polka-dotted skirt with a white jacket over a black blouse with a bow at the neck—but it wasn't in the same class of clothing as the people rushing past her.

She stepped to the side and stared out at the lake. She was here for a job interview. The position of office manager had opened up and Sofia simply couldn't keep working as a real estate agent. She needed regular hours and a regular paycheck. It was easy to say that she needed both of those things for her twins, Adelina and Eduardo, but the truth was, she needed them for herself.

Yes, this job paid enough that she could hire a nanny to help Mom out. Sofia had been a real estate agent with her husband, David. She couldn't be one without him anymore.

There were other office manager jobs she could apply for, but this one paid more. That wasn't the only reason she was here, however…

Would Eric remember her?

There was no reason he should. She hadn't seen him since he'd turned sixteen and gone away to prep school in New York. Their paths hadn't crossed in the fifteen years since and Sofia was no longer a gangly thirteen-year-old with crooked teeth.

So he wouldn't recognize her. He probably wouldn't even remember her. After all, she'd just been the daughter of the family maid and the janitor.

But she'd never forgotten him. Time might have changed her but a girl never forgot her first kiss. Even if that kiss had been the result of a dare, it still counted.

Nervously, she watched Eric's employees file in. She needed this job, but she wanted to earn it on her own merits. She didn't want to have to rely on an old family connection that he'd probably forgotten.

But desperate times and all that.

There was a lull in people exiting the elevators as she stepped forward to the reception desk. She and David had worked in a perfectly respectable office serving northern Chicago, Skokie, Lincolnwood, Evanston and the surrounding areas. But even the receptionist here had a nicer desk than she'd had at the office.

"Hello," Sofia began, projecting more confidence than she felt right now. "My name is Sofia Bingham and I have a nine a.m. interview with Mr. Jenner."

The receptionist was young, blonde and gorgeous. Her eyebrows alone were works of art, to say nothing of the trendy patterned jacket she wore. Her eyes flicked over Sofia, but she didn't so much as frown, which had to count for something. "You're here for the office manager position?" Even her voice sounded trendy.

"Yes." Confident. That was Sofia. She could handle an interview. She could handle this office—although it didn't seem to need a lot of managing.

"One moment, please." The receptionist turned her attention to her computer screen.

Sofia's stomach tightened with anxiety. She'd been selling real estate for over seven years and before that, she'd been helping at her parents' agency. But managing an office like this?

This wasn't just real estate agents. Eric Jenner no longer bought and sold houses. He bought land and built things, like this skyscraper. He employed agents and architects and interior designers and lawyers. He built exclusive office spaces and luxury apartments. And he did it so well that he had become a billionaire. Sofia didn't stalk Eric online but it'd been hard to miss when he'd been left at the altar and then, just a few months later, been named one of Chicago's top five eligible bachelors, following the marriage and subsequent delisting of his friend, Marcus Warren.

What was she even doing here? She didn't know anything about billionaires. She knew how to sell houses and condos to families, not manage architects and negotiate tax breaks with municipalities. She was struggling to hold on to middle-class respectability, for crying out loud. She'd had to move back in with her parents because she couldn't afford house payments or daycare. This was not her world.

Her chest tightened and she had trouble breathing. *Oh, no.*

No, she could not have a panic attack. Not another one, not right now. She took a step back from the reception desk, the urge to flee so strong it was almost overwhelming. Two things stopped her. The first was the image of the twins in her mother's arms this morning, all waving bye-bye to Sofia as she went off for her big interview. Mom had been training

Adelina and Eduardo to blow kisses and it was the cutest thing ever. The twins needed more than Sofia could give them right now. They needed stability and safety. They needed a mom who wasn't teetering on the edge, trying to keep everything together. To be that person for her children, she needed a steady job.

The other thing that halted her in her tracks was the sound of her name. "Ms. Bingham?"

She looked up and the air rushed out of her lungs. *There he was.* She'd seen pictures of him in those impossible-to-miss articles, but there was something unexpected about Eric Jenner in the flesh that shook her.

That smile, at least, hadn't changed. But the rest of him? Eric Jenner was now over six feet tall, moving with an easy grace that projected strength and confidence. He was simply breathtaking in a way she hadn't ever associated with him. His hair had deepened from bright copper to a rich burnished red, although his skin was still tanned. She almost grinned. Bronzed redheads were such a rare thing that it only made him all the more special.

One thing was certain—he was *not* the boy she remembered. His shoulders were broader, his legs more powerful as they closed the distance between them. And his eyes… When she lifted her gaze to his, he stumbled to a stop, his brow quirking and she knew he recognized her, even if he didn't know from where. Something in her chest loosened and she could breathe again because she knew it was going to be all right.

She hoped, anyway.

Then the realization broke over his face. *"Sofia?"* He took a step forward before pulling up short. "I'm sorry," he went on in a completely different voice. "You look like someone I used to know."

She became aware that they were standing in the middle of the reception area and that, while no one was openly staring at them, a lot of people were paying attention to this conversation. She clutched the strap of her handbag harder. "It's good to see you again, Mr. Jenner," she said because she did not want to presume anything at this point.

His face lit up and dang if that didn't make her smile. "What are you doing here? And when did you get married?" He paused and looked at her again. A warm heat flushed her cheeks. Great. Blushing.

It only got worse when he said, "Wow. You really grew up."

Her anxiety tried to wrestle control, but she powered through. "Actually, I'm your nine a.m. I'm here about the job." He blinked at her. "The opening for office manager?" she prompted him.

"Oh, oh—right." He glanced around, as if he was also just becoming aware of how this conversation might look to his employees. "This office could definitely use some management. Come on back." He cast a critical eye around and people seemed to melt back into their offices but he did so with a faint smile on his face. Sofia caught the receptionist grinning and rolling her eyes. Eric saw it, too, and said, "All right, Heather—back to work."

"Of course, Mr. Jenner," Heather the receptionist said, still smiling. She had perfectly white, perfectly even teeth, which was almost enough to distract Sofia from the sly way she winked.

Eric winked back.

Sofia's heart began to pound again. What did she know about him, really? The boy he'd been had been someone privileged and wealthy but still kind to a little girl. He'd taught her how to swim and roller-skate and had, on more than one occasion, played tea with her and some of his mother's delicate china dolls.

But that didn't mean he was the same person now. Yes, he was rich, handsome—and single. Of course he would make eyes at the beautiful young receptionist. And the beautiful young receptionist—well, she wasn't stupid. Of course she would make eyes back.

Sofia had just begun to feel invisible when Eric turned back to her. "I had no idea you were applying for this job," he said, motioning for her to follow him. "Tell me about your husband. Who was lucky enough to land Sofia Cortés?"

He said it in a way that was almost believable, the kind of benign flirting a man like Eric no doubt excelled at. But, unfortunately, it wasn't run-of-the-mill small talk to Sofia. All she could do was keep breathing.

She didn't say anything until he led her back into

his office. The room was huge, with leather couches and a massive mahogany desk, plus a wet bar. And behind it all was a wall of glass facing due east. He had an almost perfectly unobstructed view of Lake Michigan. She didn't sell downtown real estate, but even she knew this view was worth millions.

He closed the door behind her. For a moment, they stood with less than two feet separating them. Sofia became acutely aware of the heat of his body and it made her flush in a way that hadn't happened in months. Years.

"What an amazing vista," she said, striving for lighthearted—and willing him away from conversation about David. Willing away the heat she couldn't seem to ignore.

Eric Jenner was every inch the billionaire bachelor. There was no doubt in her mind that his suit was custom-made—everything he wore was probably custom-made, right down to his socks. He'd paired a bold royal blue suit with a light pink shirt and a silk tie that probably cost as much as her car payment. It all fit him like a second skin.

A forgotten feeling began to pulse through her body, a steady pounding that got louder with each beat. For a dazed moment, she didn't recognize it.

Desire. That's what this tight, hot heaviness was. *Want*. She'd forgotten she could feel this way anymore. She'd thought…well, she'd thought she'd buried her needs with her husband.

The realization that she could still feel raw attraction was startling enough. But the fact that her body was feeling desire for *Eric*? Her cheeks got hotter by the second and here in the privacy of his office, there weren't any winking receptionists or dinging elevators to distract his attention.

He stared at her, his eyes darkening. Her lungs refused to expand and she began to feel light-headed. She couldn't want Eric and he shouldn't be looking at her like that. That wasn't why she'd come.

"You've done well for yourself," she blurted out, making a conscious effort to look around the room. Photographs of him with famous people were mixed in with expensive-looking paintings and pictures of his buildings.

After a pause that was so quiet she was sure he could hear her pulse pounding, he said, "Was there any doubt?"

It sounded so cocky that she jerked back to look at him. He had a wolf's grin on his face, but then everything about him softened and she almost saw the boy she'd known. "I work hard for what I have, but let's be honest—I started from a place higher than almost everyone else, thanks to my parents."

A little bit of the anxiety loosened in her chest. Yes, he had always been the privileged son of privileged people. But the Eric she remembered had been almost embarrassed by that fact. His parents hadn't raised him to be an entitled, spoiled brat. How much of that boy still existed inside of him? Or was he the kind of man who hired a beautiful receptionist—or even a mildly attractive office manager—just to get her in bed?

She didn't want him to be like that. If he was, she wasn't sure she could destroy her fondest memories of him with reality. "How are your parents? I know they still exchange Christmas cards with my parents."

Eric sighed, an action of extreme exaggeration that made him look younger. "They're fine. They're disappointed I didn't manage to get married and start producing grandchildren, but they're fine." Before she could process that statement, he asked, "Your folks?"

"Doing well. I don't know how much your parents have shared with you, but after you went away to school, my father started selling houses. Your father opened the door for him," she added, always mindful of what the Jenners had done for her family. "It turned out there was a huge market for bilingual real estate agents and Dad was able to capitalize on that. He owns an agency in Wicker Park. Mom stays home with my children now. They spoil each other rotten."

His eyes widened before he turned away from her and strode toward his desk. Each step put physical distance between them—but there was no missing the emotional distance that went up like a wall around him.

This was all casual small talk, every bit of it. But there was something else going on that Sofia couldn't put her finger on. When he'd complained about his parents wanting grandbabies, it hadn't sounded quite right. And the look in his eyes when she'd mentioned her kids? On anyone else it would've been longing. She couldn't believe that someone like Eric Jenner, who literally had the world at his feet, would be interested in an old acquaintance's babies.

He didn't sit at the desk, didn't turn around. Instead, he stared out at the lake. Although it was still early, she could see a few boats out on the water, ready to enjoy the beautiful summer day. "I hadn't heard that you'd gotten married. Congratulations." His voice was level—unfeeling, almost.

"Oh." She couldn't help the dejected noise that escaped. Eric half turned, his silhouette outlined in sunshine. "I'm not. I mean, I was. But he…he died." No matter how long it'd been, her voice caught every time she had to state that fact out loud. "Seventeen months ago." Not that she was counting the days— the hours—since the worst day of her life.

She took a deep breath and lifted her chin. If she did this quickly, it wouldn't hurt so badly. That was the theory, anyway. "I don't know if you'd ever heard of him—David Bingham? We worked at a real estate agency up in Evanston."

He turned and took a step toward her and for a second, she thought he was going to fold her into his arms and she was going to let him. But he pulled up short. "Sofia," he said, his tone gentle. "I'm sorry. I had no idea. How are you doing?"

That wasn't small talk. That was an honest question from one of her oldest friends. God, she'd missed Eric.

It was so tempting to lie and smooth over the awkward moment with platitudes. Lord knew Eric was probably looking for an easy answer.

But none of her answers were easy. "That's why I'm here. My twins are—"

"Twins?" he cut her off, his eyes bugging out of his head. "How old?"

"Fifteen months."

He let out a low whistle of appreciation as his gaze traveled the length of her body. Her cheeks warmed at his leisurely inspection but then his face shuttered again. "I can't even imagine how difficult that must have been for you. I'm so sorry for your loss."

"I…thank you. It's been hard. Which," she went on before he could distract her from her purpose again with his kind eyes and kinder words, "is why I'm here. David and I sold houses together and since he passed I just…can't. I need a job with regular hours and a steady paycheck to provide for my children." There. She'd gotten her spiel out and it'd only hurt a little.

"What are their names?"

"Adelina and Eduardo, although I call them Addy and Eddy—which my mom hates." She pulled her phone out of her handbag and called up the most recent picture, of the twins in the bath with matching grins, wet hair sticking straight up. "They're officially toddlers now. Mom watches them but I think she's outnumbered most days. I'd love to hire a nanny to help out." And pay off the bills that were piling up and put a little away for the kids' college funds and...

The list of problems money would solve for her was long. Even at the best of times, real estate involved odd hours and an unpredictable income. But if an agent couldn't sell a house without sobbing in the car, then the income got very predictable. Zero.

Eric took the phone. She watched him carefully as he tilted the screen and studied their little faces. "They look like you," he said. "Beautiful."

Her face flushed at the sincere compliment. "Thank you. They've kept me going."

Because if she hadn't had two helpless little babies that needed to be fed and rocked and loved, she might've curled into a ball and given up. The numbing depression and crushing panic attacks were never far, but Addy and Eddy were more than just her children. They were David's children—all she had left of him. She couldn't let him down. She couldn't let herself down.

So she'd kept moving forward—one day, one hour, sometimes even just one minute at a time. It'd gotten easier. That didn't make it easy, though.

Eric stared at the shot of her babies for a long moment before finally motioning Sofia to one of the plush leather seats before his desk. "And you want to try your hand at office management? This isn't a typical real estate office."

She lifted her chin again. "Mr. Jenner—"

"Eric, Sofia. We know each other too well for formalities, don't you think?" It was a challenge, the way he said it. "I'm not sure I could think of you as Mrs. Bingham, anyway. You'll always be Sofia Cortés to me."

She understood because she wanted to keep him as that fun, sweet boy in her mind forever. But she couldn't afford to romanticize the potential billionaire employer sitting behind his executive desk and she couldn't afford to let him romanticize her.

"That's who I was," she said, her words coming out more gently than she meant for them to. "But that's not who I am now. We've grown up, you and I. We're not the same kids splashing in the pool we used to be and I *need* this job."

His gaze met hers and she saw something there that she didn't want to think too deeply about. "Then it's yours."

Two

This was a mistake. Eric knew it before the words had left his mouth. But by then, it was too late.

He had just offered the position of office manager to a woman he wasn't entirely sure was qualified.

That was true, but it wasn't the whole truth. Because it wasn't some random woman off the street. It was Sofia Cortés. He'd practically grown up with her.

But this wasn't the little girl he remembered from his childhood. The woman before him was—well, she was all grown up. Despite the suit jacket and skirt she wore, Eric couldn't help but notice her body. Sofia was a woman in every sense. She came almost to his chin, her thick black hair pulled away from her face. Eric had an unreasonable urge to sink his fingers into her hair and tilt her head to the side, exposing the long line of her neck.

He shook that thought out of his head. Why hadn't his mother told him Sofia had gotten married and had twins, much less that her husband had died? Surely Mom knew. If nothing else, those were the sorts of things that tended to make a Christmas newsletter.

"Are you… Are you sure?" Sofia asked, looking stunned.

Eric felt much the same. He always did a thorough investigation of a candidate's skills. Even when he knew he wanted to hire them anyway, like Heather for the position of receptionist. Not only did she have the perfect look for the face of his company, but she was finishing her MBA on the company's dime. He hadn't hired her just because she was hot, although that never hurt. He'd hired her because she was brilliant and would transition into the contracts department. It was never too early to begin building loyalty and Eric's staff was beyond loyal.

That was something he'd learned from his father. Nurture the best talent and pay them well and they'd fight for you. Wasn't that why Sofia was here? Because the Jenner family had supported the Cortés family?

"Of course," he said with a certainty he wasn't sure was warranted. "Can you do the job?"

The color deepened along her cheeks. He was *not* going to notice how pretty it was on her. She didn't look like a widow with two adorable young children.

She looked…*lush*. And tempting.

He would not be tempted. One of his hard and fast rules was that he didn't hit on staff. Flirt, maybe. But he never put a valued employee in a position where they felt they couldn't say no because he was the boss.

What a shame he was hiring Sofia, then. Because that would put her completely out of reach. Which was fine. Good. She was undoubtedly still struggling with being a widow and a single mother. She didn't need the complications that seemed to follow Eric like shadows cast by the afternoon sun.

Sofia cleared her throat. "I'm a quick study. I helped run my dad's office when I was in school and staged homes part-time in college. I've been selling ever since I graduated." She dropped her gaze and cleared her throat. "Until…"

What had she said? Seventeen months since she had been left a widow. And her twins—two of the cutest babies he had ever seen—were fifteen months old.

Eric's world was one of logic and calculation. Real estate was a gamble on the best of days. But he always weighed the pros and cons of any option and he never bet more than he could afford to lose.

Of course, as a billionaire, he could afford to lose a lot.

Somehow, none of the usual checks and balances weighed much with this decision. Sofia was an old friend. Her family were good people. And those babies…

"The job is yours. There'll be a learning curve, I'm sure, but I'm confident you'll pick it up." Either Sofia would or she wouldn't. He had to give her that chance. And if she didn't, then he'd help her find a position that better fit her skill set. Something with regular hours and a paycheck that would help her raise her toddlers by herself. And if that happened… then she wouldn't work for him, would she? He could get to know her all over again. Every inch of her.

Hell. He was not thinking about Sofia—not like that. Especially because he was still hiring her. It was the right thing to do.

Her eyes were huge, but she managed a smile. "That's…that's wonderful."

"We have a generous benefits package," he went on, pulling a number out of thin air. "The starting salary is a hundred and twenty thousand a year, with bonuses based on performance. Is it enough?"

Her mouth dropped open and she looked at him as if she'd never seen him before. He could afford to pay well because hiring the best people was worth it in the long run. But he honestly couldn't tell from her expression if she was insulted by that amount or flabbergasted.

"You can't be serious," she said in a strangled voice.

Eric raised an eyebrow at her. A couple extra

thousand for him was nothing. Pocket change. "How about a hundred and forty-five?"

She got alarmingly pale. "Your negotiation skills are rusty," she finally croaked out, a hand pressed to her chest. "You're not supposed to go up, certainly not by twenty-five thousand. A hundred and twenty is enough. More than enough."

Eric cracked a grin at her. "And your negotiation skills…" He trailed off, shaking his head in mock disapproval. "That would've been the point to say make it one fifty and it's a deal. Are you sure you sold houses?" She got even paler and he realized teasing her was not the smartest thing to do. In fact, she looked like she was on the verge of fainting. "Are you all right?" He moved to the wet bar and grabbed a bottle of sparkling water. She was breathing heavily by the time he made his way back to her. "Sofia?"

He set the water on the desk and put his fingers on the side of her neck. Her pulse fluttered weakly under his touch and her skin was clammy. "Breathe," he ordered, pushing her head down toward her knees. He crouched next to her. "Sofia? Honey, *breathe*."

They sat like that for several minutes while he rubbed her back and tried his best to sound soothing. What the hell had happened? Normally, when he offered people more money, they jumped to say yes.

But this woman had actually tried to say no.

He focused on smoothing her hair away from her forehead, on how her muscles tensed and relaxed along her spine as he rubbed her back. Even through her jacket, he could feel the warmth of her body. He couldn't imagine touching anyone else like this.

She was still struggling for air. Was this a medical crisis? He felt for her pulse again. It was steady enough. He needed to distract her. "Remember the sailboat races?" he asked. But he didn't pull his hand away from her. He stayed close.

"Yes," she said softly. "You let me win sometimes."

"Let you? Come on, Sofia. You beat me fair and square."

Her head popped up, a shaky grin on her face. "You're being kind," she said, her voice strangely quiet.

Eric realized there was less than a foot between them. If he wanted to kiss her, all he'd have to do was lean forward.

It came back to him in a rush—he'd kissed her once before, when they were kids. He'd had Marcus Warren over and Marcus had dared Eric to kiss her. So he had. And she'd let him.

Somehow, Eric knew that if he kissed her now, it wouldn't be a timid touching of lips. This time, he'd taste her, dipping his tongue into her mouth and savoring her sweetness. He'd take possession of her mouth and, God willing, she'd...

He jerked back so quickly he almost landed on his butt. "Here," he said gruffly, snagging the bottle of water off his desk and wrenching the cap off.

What the hell was wrong with him? He couldn't

be thinking about Sofia Cortés like that. It didn't matter that she wasn't the same innocent little kid. It didn't even matter that she'd been married and had children. He couldn't think of her like that.

He'd just hired her.

She took the water but didn't look him in the eye. "I didn't realize how expensive those toy boats were until we sank the loser that one time. Which was me, of course."

"You were a worthy opponent but that avalanche was unavoidable," he replied. He barely remembered the boat. But he did remember the sheer glee when they'd hit the boat with a decorative stone so large it'd taken both of them to toss it. The splash had been *huge*. "You have to admit it was fun."

That got her to meet his gaze. "How old were we? I still remember the horror in my mom's eyes when she caught us."

"I was ten, I think. Old enough to know better, I was informed." His parents had been more than a little exasperated with him, but his dad hadn't been able to stop snickering when Eric had described the rockslide. "It was only a couple hundred dollars. No big deal."

Well, that and his parents had made him get every single rock out of the pool. His mother was of the opinion that they didn't need the pool boy to suffer for Eric's foolishness. Still, it had taken three people to get the boulder out of the deep end.

Sofia rolled her eyes at him, which made him

grin. "Maybe to you. My mother was horrified that we'd have to pay it back somehow." She was talking to him now, sounding more like the Sofia he remembered. "There was no way we could have afforded that. Not then."

"That's why I took the blame." He leaned against the desk, his arms crossed over his chest. He wished they weren't in this office. He'd give anything to be out on the lake this morning. There, with the sun on his face and the wind in his hair, he'd be able to think clearly. Here, his mind was muddled.

She looked at him again. Her color was better and she seemed…well, not like the girl he'd known. But maybe someone he could still be friends with.

Friends who didn't kiss, that was.

"You always were," she murmured before she took another deep drink of the water.

"Were what?"

"Kind. One of the kindest people I'd ever known." She dropped her gaze. "You still are. This job…" She swallowed.

Kind? This wasn't kind. This was calculated. He was building loyalty and ensuring morale. This was keeping an eye on his business. And if it didn't work out, well—he'd show her *kind*. He'd have her out of her buttoned-up jacket and skirt so fast her head would spin.

He laughed at his own thoughts, a bitter sound. "I'm not. I'm ruthless. A coldhearted bastard of the first order. Don't you read the headlines?"

Three

Eric stared at her for a long moment, a dare in his eyes. Then he turned away and went to admire his view of the lake. The way he looked, silhouetted against the window, his shoulders broad and his hair curling gently just above the collar of his shirt—to say nothing of his backside in those custom-made pants...

She had seen the headlines, of course. He'd been left at the altar. He'd been named one of the "Top Five Billionaire Bachelors of Chicago." He'd been ruthless in his business dealings. But none of that was who he really was.

Was it?

Even if life had changed them both, she knew that deep down, they were still the same people they'd been back when they'd been kids. He wasn't a heart-less bastard, no matter what people might say.

Heartless bastards wouldn't have rubbed her back when she'd had a panic attack. They wouldn't have gotten her water. They would have laughed her and her crippling anxiety right out of the office and slammed the door in her face.

Heartless bastards wouldn't have looked like they were going to kiss her and they most certainly wouldn't have stopped at just a look.

At least, Sofia thought that's what Eric had been thinking. She hadn't been kissed in a long time so she couldn't be sure. She and David had enjoyed a passionate four years together before she'd gotten pregnant. But after her body had begun to change, so had their love life. The intimacy had been deeper, richer—but at the cost of some of the heat.

She fanned herself. It was unnaturally warm in here.

"Are you sure you want me to work for you? Good office managers don't have panic attacks."

"Of course they do," he answered without turning around. "They just choose their locations wisely. I've always found it's best to have a panic attack safely behind closed doors. No one wants to pass out next to the coffeepot." He glanced back at her with a smirk. "Location, location, location—right?"

"Eric…"

A ripple of tension rolled over his shoulders. "Does that happen a lot?"

"It's...better." How to answer this question without making it sound like she was incapable of doing the job? "They started after David collapsed. One of them actually triggered early labor, but they got it stopped in time and I was on bed rest for five weeks. I hadn't had one in a few months, though. I just wasn't expecting any offer to be that..."

"Generous?"

"Insane." This was the first time an attack had been triggered by something positive. "Eric, I can't take that much money. The position was for seventy thousand. You can't just randomly double it because we used to be friends."

He made a scoffing sound and at that moment, he did sound a little ruthless. "First off, we're still friends and second off, I absolutely can. Who's going to stop me?"

A hundred and twenty was slightly more than she and David had earned together in a single year. The things she could do with that kind of money... but she didn't want to be Eric's charity case. "Most comparable positions are fifty to sixty thousand," she protested.

That made him snort. "Comparable to what, Sofia? If you're saying this position is just like running your suburban brokerage, you couldn't be more wrong. I can promise you regular hours most of the time, but I'll expect you to travel to potential sites occasionally. This isn't just ordering paper clips and deciding how ten agents divide them. I employ forty lawyers, architects, agents, tax specialists, lobbyists—"

"Lobbyists?" The fact that she had no idea why he would have lobbyists on staff was probably a sign that she was in over her head.

"To negotiate with municipalities and influence laws, of course. We're pursuing a project in St. Louis as we speak. If we play our cards right, we'll get tax breaks from the city, county and state." He grinned like he'd won the lottery.

"Of course," she mumbled, unsure what else she was supposed to say. He was right. She was vastly out of her league.

"Besides," he continued, sounding more than just a little cold as he turned his attention back out the window, "what's a spare fifty thousand or so to a guy like me?"

Nothing, probably. She could see how that wouldn't bankrupt a billionaire. Still, though. It was the principle of the matter. "But—"

"By the way," he went on, as if she hadn't spoken, "I have a better boat now. You should come with me sometime. I like to sail in the afternoons."

He still wasn't looking at her, but it was clear from the tone of his voice that the conversation about salary was finished.

"Is it a sailboat?" she asked.

"Nope. It's a yacht. And we won't sink this one with a rock, so don't worry. You could…" He paused and then continued, "You could even bring the kids. I bet they'd love being out on the water."

What was happening here? Eric was giving her a job and paying her way too much money. And now he was inviting her boating? With two rambunctious toddlers in tow? "Eric…"

"Never mind. I hear you've got a real bastard of a boss who won't let you take off work just to go jetting around." He turned and she barely recognized him at all—his face was that hard. "Come on. Let's find out what you've gotten yourself into, shall we?"

More than she could handle, she thought as she followed him to the door of his office and into the heart of Jenner Properties.

Three hours later, Sofia knew she was in over her head. She was reasonably confident Eric knew it, too—but it didn't seem to bother him. He would give her a look and say, "All right?" as if he were willing it to be true instead of asking a question.

He was putting a lot of faith in her and she didn't want to let him down. She didn't want to let her mom or her kids down, either. But most of all, she needed to do this for herself. This was the first big change she had undertaken on her own since her life had been thrown into upheaval a year and a half ago. She was tired of life happening to her. She was going to happen to her life. This job was the first step.

Even if that meant she would have to make it up as she went along.

"And here are Meryl and Steve Norton," Eric was saying as he knocked on the last door to the office closest to his. "Meryl is my chief negotiator for the St. Louis project and Steve is the project manager. It helps that they're married," he added in a stage whisper. "Guys, this is Sofia Bingham. She's our new office manager."

"Hello," Sofia said, smiling. Eric had stopped accidentally saying Cortés after only five or six introductions.

"Welcome," a tall, jovial man with thinning hair said as he rose from a desk on one side of the office. He was a little soft around the middle, but his smile was friendly and his eyes were warm. "To the madhouse," he went on, shaking her hand. "I'm Steve. I handle contractors."

As big as Steve was, an equally tiny woman hopped down off her desk chair from the other side of the room. Steve slid his arm around her shoulders as Meryl Norton said, "Don't listen to him. It's not that bad—as long as you can embrace the madness. I'm Meryl and I handle politicians. If you have any questions, don't hesitate to ask. I'm generally friendly." But she said it in such a way that Sofia couldn't help but grin in response.

Eric's wristwatch dinged and he said, "I've got to take this. Sofia, when you're done catching up with the Nortons, ask Heather to show you where all the supplies are. If I'm still here when you're done, stop in and see me. If not, check in with Tonya. She'll have your contract." With that, he was gone.

Sofia had done all right by his side because everyone in this building deferred to him. Eric seemed to understand his staff not just as employees but as people. Eric had given her a heads-up for the introverts who needed quiet to focus and the extroverts who needed someone to help them stay on task.

And Steve Norton clearly was an extrovert. "There's a rumor going around that you and the big boss used to know each other," he began with no other introduction, a slightly mischievous gleam in his eye.

"Honey," Meryl said, elbowing him. If she hadn't been so small, she would've elbowed him in the ribs. As it was, she more or less hit him in the hip bone. "Don't pry. He pries," she went on, giving Sofia a sympathetic look. "Did Mr. Jenner explain that there'll be times when travel is a part of the job?"

"He did—and," she added, before Steve could ask again, "we did know each other when we were little kids. His father gave my father his start in real estate." Normally, she might not have revealed that. But it was better to clarify up front that she and Eric had never dated or otherwise had any romantic entanglements. In an office of this size, gossip could make her life a living hell. "Our parents still send Christmas cards to each other."

Steve looked amused by this. Meryl said to her husband, "There. Now you don't have to pry anymore. We're planning a trip to St. Louis next month," she went on, turning back to Sofia without pausing for breath. "They recently lost their football team and there's a section of the downtown that's depressed. We wouldn't expect you to be involved in negotiations, but planning trips like this would be your responsibility. So far, Heather and I have been handling this together, but I think it would be a good idea for you to join us. That way, in the future, you'll know how Mr. Jenner likes things done. You do have a background in real estate, correct?"

"I've been in real estate since I was fourteen. However, this is a different level," she admitted. Okay, she could handle a business trip with Eric. No problem.

"That's why the St. Louis trip will be good," Meryl said decisively. She definitely talked like a negotiator. "You get a chance to see what Mr. Jenner is trying to accomplish when he branches out into smaller markets and how you can help make that happen. Understanding the business is key to understanding how the office works."

Sofia glanced at Steve. For the project manager, he wasn't doing a lot of talking. He looked like he wanted to ask her something else that was probably personal, but Meryl plowed ahead. "I'll email you the current itinerary. We look forward to working with you, but no one expects you to manage Steve. That's my job," she added with a wink.

Steve protested loudly, although Sofia could tell

it was all for show. Meryl waved Sofia away—but as she shut the door behind her, they were both laughing.

Sofia stood for a moment on the other side of the door, trying to get her bearings. She'd expected the interview to last an hour, if that—but she'd been here for almost four hours. Mom would worry, although the situation wouldn't get desperate until the twins got up from their naps. They had just come through a protracted period of clinginess and it was still touch and go when Addy and Eddy were waking up.

Eric's office was to the right of Steve and Meryl's. His door was closed. There was a window to the left. It didn't have a sweeping view of Lake Michigan, but it was no hardship to look at the Chicago skyline.

She stepped into a warm shaft of afternoon sunlight and checked her messages. Mom had texted a photo of the twins destroying their lunch. Sofia's heart clenched as she looked at her babies. When she and David had discovered they were having twins, she'd planned to take time off after their birth. She'd even entertained the notion of a maternity leave that lasted several years. But the life insurance policy had run out and honestly, as overwhelming as today had been, it'd been nice to have a conversation without someone screaming.

She replied to the text message with what time she thought she'd be home and then paused to look at the office.

It was spotless and gleaming. Eric's executive

suite had been practically a temple to wealth and privilege, but even the carpet in the general areas was thick and plush. The office equipment she'd glanced at was state-of-the-art, and he provided snacks and beverages to everyone, not just coffee. Eric didn't cheap out on providing for his employees.

This office—this job—represented so much for her. There was more to her than life as a widow and mother of two babies.

Eric Jenner was giving her the opportunity to be more.

She worked her way around the front of the office, where trendy Heather was still behind the receptionist desk. "Um, hello. Mr. Jenner told me to—"

She cut Sofia off without even looking up. "One moment." Sofia swallowed. After a minute that felt painfully long, Heather finished whatever she was doing and stood, straightening her jacket. She had shimmering golden hair that fell halfway down her back. She was so young and effortlessly beautiful that Sofia couldn't help but feel old and fat by comparison.

"The supply closet is this way." Heather led Sofia back to a closet tucked behind the emergency stairwell. When they were inside with the door mostly shut behind them Heather turned to her. She cast a critical eye at Sofia's outfit again. "I don't know if anyone has said this to you yet," she began and Sofia braced herself. *Here it comes*, she thought. Heather went on, "But we're really glad you're here."

Sofia's mouth dropped open in shock. "I'm sorry?" Of all the things she'd expected Heather to say, an expression of welcome hadn't made the list. "You are?"

"Oh my gosh, yes. Stacy—the previous office manager? She got married and had a baby and decided she wanted to be a stay-at-home mom. Mr. Jenner offered me the job? But I'm almost done with my MBA and he's already promised me a job in the contracts department. I've been doing this job *and* the receptionist job *and* training for the contracts department while finishing up my schooling and it's exhausting. I'm beyond thrilled to hand the reins over to you," she said and her smile seemed surprisingly genuine.

Sofia realized she had misjudged the young woman. Just because she was pretty and fashionable didn't mean Heather was catty or vain. "Do you like working for him?" Because Sofia had not forgotten those cheeky winks. "I mean, what kind of boss is he?"

"The best boss? I mean, really. The company is paying for my MBA. They already put my fiancée on the benefits package and we're not even married yet?" She had this habit of ending her statements on an up note, as if she were asking a question. "You'd think that a billionaire like him would be a total jerk, but he's actually really down-to-earth. The benefits package alone is worth this job? Everything else is just icing on the cake."

Fiancé. Sofia took a deep breath and smiled widely. "Congratulations on your engagement. What's his name?"

Heather slanted her a sly smile. "Her name is Suzanne."

Sofia felt her cheeks go bright red. "Oh, I'm sorry. I didn't mean to assume. It's just that…" Well, there had been those winks.

"Oh, no worries," Heather said, waving away Sofia's embarrassment. "It's a known fact that Mr. Jenner flirts with everyone. He's an equal opportunity flirt. But he keeps a hard line between flirting and hitting on someone." She leaned forward, her voice quieting to a whisper. "We're not supposed to talk about his former fiancée—and I don't recommend bringing it up—but there was a young woman who'd just started in the agent department when Mr. Jenner got dumped. She made a move."

It was wrong to gossip about Eric, both as an old friend and a new boss. That noble sentiment didn't stop Sofia from asking, "And?"

"And not only did he rebuff her advances, she was gone a month later."

"He *fired* her?"

"No, actually. That's the weird thing." Heather looked just as confused as Sofia felt. "She got 'a better offer' from one of his business rivals. The rumor is Mr. Jenner engineered it. I overheard him tell the Nortons that Wyatt got what he deserved out of the deal."

Wyatt—hadn't there been a kid named Robert Wyatt back when they were kids? If she was thinking of the same boy, then that was the kid who'd cornered her one time while Eric had been in the bathroom and tried to cop a feel.

Sofia remembered she'd done what her father had taught her and kneed Wyatt hard in the groin. Eric had found his so-called friend rolling on the ground and yelling bloody murder and Sofia had been terrified Wyatt would get her mom fired. But instead, Wyatt never came back over to play and Mrs. Jenner had bought Sofia a doll with a new set of clothes.

Heather was staring intently at her. "Well. That's…interesting, isn't it?" Sofia said numbly.

If she'd thought that would be the end of the conversation, she was wrong. "You two used to know each other?" Heather, Sofia realized, was the office gossip. Which meant that she was a good person to have on Sofia's side. But that didn't mean she wanted to spread every childhood moment she and Eric had shared around the office. There was a fine line here and Sofia had to figure out how to walk it—quickly.

When she didn't answer right away, Heather pressed on. "I mean, that's what it sounded like. I've never heard him tell an interviewee—or anyone else, for that matter—that they 'grew up.'"

"We knew each other when we were little kids. His father gave my father a start in business." That line had worked well enough for the Nortons, but when Heather didn't respond immediately, Sofia decided she needed to steer the conversation away from the past. "It's good to hear that he's still the same kid he used to be. I was hoping being a billionaire hadn't changed him."

Heather exhaled heavily. "I don't think the money is what's changed him," she said quietly. Then she turned a too-bright smile to Sofia. "Okay? Here are the vendors that we use to order coffee…"

Sofia didn't get the chance to ask what Heather meant by that. And did it matter, really? No. What mattered was that Eric was giving her an incredible opportunity and putting a great deal of faith in her. What mattered was that his staff loved working for him. What mattered more than anything, she decided, was that he didn't sleep with his receptionist and he nurtured the talents of the people he hired.

She was going to make this work, she decided with renewed resolve.

So she better learn how to order the coffee.

Four

Normally, Eric would've been on the water by now. There was only one reason he was still at his desk today. *Sofia*. Somehow, he couldn't leave without making sure she'd take the job.

He was supposed to be reading her contract and nondisclosure agreement, but it wasn't going well. He was also supposed to be looking over the latest plans for the St. Louis trip, but he wasn't doing that, either.

Instead, he was thinking about Sofia. He couldn't remember the first time he'd seen her. She'd always been there. There hadn't been any big formal goodbyes, either. The Cortés family had not come to his farewell party when he'd gone away to school. He hadn't sought her out after the party. That had been that.

She'd always been a part of his life—until she wasn't anymore. He wanted to think he'd regretted not getting the closure of a goodbye, but honestly, he wasn't sure he had.

Now suddenly Sofia was back in his life. A mother with two little babies who depended on her.

She was taking the job, by God. That was final.

A soft knock on his door pulled him out of his messy thoughts. "Yes?"

The door opened and there she was. His breath caught in his throat as she stepped into his office. It didn't seem possible that she got lovelier every time he saw her.

But there was no denying it—she was simply prettier than she'd been an hour ago. Especially when her eyes lit up as she looked at him, her mouth softening into a kissable smile. "You're still here," she said, a touch of wonder in her voice. "I thought you'd be out on the lake by now."

He grinned. It didn't mean anything that she remembered how much he needed the water. Everyone else thought it was part of his eccentric charm, but Sofia had always understood that he needed the water like some people needed the air. "I'm still here," he told her. "Have a seat. I'm just going over your contract."

He watched her carefully as she crossed the room and sat in front of him. She looked a little bashful, but not like she was on the verge of another anxiety attack. "I don't suppose you made my salary something reasonable?"

"A hundred and twenty thousand is very reasonable, Sofia."

She laughed. "What if I'm not worth that much money?"

He was stunned by the words—and by how much she seemed to mean them. Nervously, she glanced up at him. "I'm going to pretend you didn't say that," he said. "Stop acting like you don't belong here."

"I don't," she said, and he was impressed that she didn't sound cowed when she said it. "You're the one trying to make me fit into this world."

"You're the one who showed up for a job interview," he reminded her. At that, she opened her mouth to reply and then closed it with an audible snap. "There. We agree. You want the job and I'm giving it to you." He shoved the contract across the desk.

She reached for it, and he continued, "It's the standard contract, details on the benefit plan, bonus schedule and nondisclosure agreement. You're more than welcome to take it home and look it over. If you decide to accept the job, I'd like you to start next week. But Sofia?" She looked up at him again, the contract in her hand. "You're going to accept the job."

He braced for the worst—another panic attack—but it didn't happen. Instead, her brows furrowed and she twisted her lips. "I'm not going to win this argument, am I?"

"Of course not. I never lose arguments when I happen to be right."

"What are you going to tell your parents?"

He blinked once, then again. Of all the things she might have said—that wasn't what he'd expected. "I don't know that I need to tell them anything." Except that was a hedge and he knew it.

Because he wanted to know why his mother hadn't kept him up-to-date on what Sofia was doing and there was no way he could ask without revealing that Sofia now worked for him.

"I assume your parents know where you are?" he asked.

"They do." She dropped her gaze back to the contract and flipped the page. "They were worried."

"About?" Suddenly, he found himself hoping the Cortés family hadn't followed all the headlines—his abandonment on his wedding day or the subsequent re-sowing of his wild oats afterward.

"They want to see me succeed but...well, they knew this job was a stretch for me. I don't have the experience." She looked up at him and he saw the truth in her eyes. "I shouldn't even be telling you this," she went on in a rush. "Because the truth is that we're not friends anymore. We're old acquaintances who only knew each other because my parents worked for yours. Now you're my boss and I shouldn't be telling you about my family's hopes or that I suffered debilitating panic attacks after my husband died. You're not supposed to know these things about me."

She was almost shouting at him. The force of her emotion pushed him back in his chair.

"Oh, God," she said, slumping down. "And I definitely shouldn't be yelling at you. I couldn't be screwing this up more if I tried, could I?"

If it were anyone else, he'd agree. He'd show her the door and count himself lucky to have dodged a bullet.

So why wasn't he doing that right now?

When was the last time anyone had put him in his place? No one—with the obvious exception of his parents—talked to him like this. They all minced around him like he was a volatile chemical and they were afraid of the reaction he'd spark. Even Marcus Warren—who had no trouble telling anyone what he thought about anything—had been pulling his punches with Eric.

Sofia telling him off should have been infuriating. But...

All he could think about was how he'd missed her. And how he hoped she'd missed him, too. "You need a friend."

She looked at him, her eyes suspiciously shiny and a quirky smile on her face. "Maybe you do, too." Abruptly, she stood, grabbing her handbag and clutching the contract to her chest. "I'm going to take this job because you're right, I need it. But I won't be your object of pity. You don't owe me a larger salary. You don't owe me any special perks. I'm your employee. Try to remember that."

That was, hands down, one of the most effective set-downs he'd ever received in his life. It was so good that all he could do was smile as she walked out of the office.

"Mama!" Two small voices cried in unison when Sofia came through the door that evening. She still felt that she was moving in a daze but at least here, in the sanctuary of her parents' house, with her two children launching themselves at her, everything still felt the same.

"Babies!" she cried back, just like she did every time she had to be away from them. She opened her arms as they flung themselves at her, almost knocking her off balance in her heeled shoes. "Were you good for Abuelita today?" she asked over their heads as her mother slowly climbed to her feet from where she'd been sitting on the floor.

"Fine, fine," Mom said, waving away this concern. "How about you? You got the job?" Then, after a moment's hesitation, she added, "Did he remember you?"

Sofia staggered over to the couch that was possibly older than she was with the children squirming in her arms, collapsing in a heap of happy baby sounds. Addy curled up in her lap and began humming contentedly while Eddy slid down and toddled over to a small set of table and chairs, where he picked up a piece of paper he'd made some very colorful lines on. He showed it to her proudly.

"Oh," Sofia said, touching the picture. "So pretty." Eddy began to chatter about whatever it was he'd drawn. She grinned. The twins weren't quite talking yet, but they sure had a lot to say.

As expected, Addy took all this attention for Eddy as a direct challenge to her artistic merits. She went to get her drawing, too. The twins were always competing like this and only occasionally did it result in tears.

After she had also complimented Addy's colorful lines, she leaned back, settling into the ancient cushions of the couch while the twins started coloring again. Even when her father had started selling houses and they'd moved into this small ranch home, the Cortéses hadn't wasted any money on new furniture.

Even though they were now respectably middle class, they still lived carefully and those were lessons Sofia had a hard time unlearning. It'd taken a long time to get used to the way David would decide he wanted a new phone or a new computer and just go buy it. Almost all of their fights had been about money. She'd never felt comfortable spending it but he couldn't understand why she didn't want a few nice things.

If anything, Eric was a million times worse than David ever could have been. The craziest thing David had ever done with money—besides spending five thousand dollars on her engagement ring—had been buying a brand-new, top-of-the-line flat screen television that took up a huge chunk of wall in their living room. But that had only been seven thousand dollars.

Eric was throwing an extra *fifty* thousand dollars at her. Truly, he was being an idiot about it. But wasn't she being an idiot to try to give that cash back? It wasn't like she couldn't use the money. The life insurance money had run out and she'd moved back in with her parents because, well, she'd been in the grips of depression and the mother of two newborns. But it'd also been to save money.

She sighed. Eric was right. Fifty thousand was a year to her. To him, it couldn't be more than fifteen minutes of one day. And she had shown up for the job interview hoping that the Jenner kindness would help her get back on her feet. She was in no position to refuse that kindness.

Her mother appeared with a glass of lemonade and a worried smile on her face. "Well?"

"He remembered me. And I got the job." She took the lemonade and drank deeply. "He's paying me too much money."

At this, Mom smiled. "The Jenners—they always pay too much. They're very generous people."

Sofia looked up at her mother. Rosa Cortés had worked her entire life to take care of Sofia. But it wasn't until Sofia had unexpectedly become a widow with two infants that she had appreciated how her mother always kept her head up and hope in her heart.

Mom had given her everything. It was time for Sofia to return the favor. "Listen, I'm going to start paying you to watch the kids. And hire someone to help out."

Her mother's eyes got wide and then immediately narrowed. Sofia braced herself. "You'll do no such thing," she snapped. "I love spending the day with my *nietos*. It's not a job."

"Yes, I will." Sofia was almost too tired to argue—but this was important. "You quit your job at the brokerage to stay home with us. You've kept me going more times than I can count. You've always taken care of me, Mom. Let me take care of you, too."

Her mother shook her head and stamped her foot, which was a show of temper for her. Rosa was so mild mannered as to be meek.

"Fine," Sofia said, knowing further debate would only make Mom dig in her heels even more. "I'll put the money in a retirement account for you. And I will hire someone to help out. That's nonnegotiable. You know Dad's going to be on my side about this."

Although he would never want to hurt Mom's feelings by suggesting she couldn't do everything, Dad had privately told Sofia he worried the twins might be too much for Mom.

Her mother looked like she was going to argue

but just then, Addy flung her crayons to the side and stared at Sofia's glass, moving her hands in the way that meant she wanted some, too. Not to be outdone, Eddy plopped his bottom down on the rug and began to fuss. Mom clucked softly. "Oh, now—you two, it's time to wash our hands and have a snack." She picked up Eddy and Addy toddled along behind, the mention of a snack suddenly the most important thing in the world.

Sofia grinned after her babies. She had pictures of David at that age and Eddy, especially, was going to look a lot like his father. Addy's hair was a little darker, her face a little more round—just like Sofia's had been.

She sank back into the old couch, grateful for the moment of silence. Maybe her mother was right. Maybe that's all there was to this insane salary. Eric was just being generous. Maybe it had nothing to do with her at all. To a guy like him, a Jenner, money was the easy, obvious solution. It would never run out.

It didn't feel like that, though. If anything, it felt... dangerous. More than just the way he'd talked her down from the panic attack, more than the heated way he looked at her whenever she pushed back against his dictates. Those things were bad enough, but easy to dismiss as old friends catching up or him flirting with her just like he flirted with everyone else.

No, what was dangerous to Sofia's mental well-being was the way he had matter-of-factly stated that he could somehow keep her safe.

It had been a sweet thing to say, but Sofia had recognized something else in his eyes when he said it, something lost. He had been left at the altar. Had he loved his ex-fiancée? Had his whole world changed in that one single moment and he still wasn't sure who he'd become in the aftermath?

How far had he fallen before he'd picked himself back up?

She shook her head. It didn't matter. She couldn't be that friend for him, not like in the old days. She was a professional. And besides, she didn't have much of a heart left to be broken.

"What am I supposed to do, David?" she whispered in the quiet of the room. She got no answer, but she wasn't expecting one.

She had the job. She could take care of her outstanding bills, hire some help for her mom and start moving past living just one day at a time. And she could do all that without getting entangled in Eric's life again. She'd keep a tight handle on any behavior that might be construed as unprofessional, too. No more panic attacks—at least not in public. No more telling him she wasn't qualified for the job. She didn't belong in his world, but she could fake it until she made it.

The job was hers. She would do it for her children and her parents.

But most of all, she would do the job for herself. She needed the work and the salary.

She just had to remember that she didn't need Eric.

Five

"Darling!" Elise Jenner said from behind her desk in her office in the mansion. Dad's was connected to hers with a door, but they kept it firmly shut. Mom lived in mortal terror that John Jenner's clutter would spread like a contagion through the house.

His mother's office was best described as Louis XVI run amok. Rococo flourishes, gilt trim and pink upholstery made the place almost blinding to look at. Everything about Elise Jenner was overdone. Eric might not decorate with gold leaf, but his buildings had been described as over-the-top on more than one occasion. At least he came by it honestly.

"We weren't expecting you tonight." She studied him as he kicked off his shoes before stepping on the Persian rug. That had been a rule in this house for as long as he could remember. "What's wrong?"

"Why didn't you tell me that Sofia Cortés got married? Or widowed? Or had twins?"

His mother looked at him, surprised. "Why, dear—I didn't think you remembered her. You never asked about her." She sat back, looking perturbed. "What brought this on?"

"How could I forget her?" he replied, avoiding this second question. "She was practically my best friend when we were kids. Something I recall you encouraging," he added.

Elise tilted her head and stared at him. For all of her love of extravagant interior design, the woman wasn't soft. She cultivated a flamboyant image and then used it ruthlessly to her advantage. "What happened today, dear?"

Coming to visit his parents in this mood was a mistake. He wanted answers—not an interrogation. But the day with Sofia had muddled his thinking. "I hired her today. She's my new office manager."

"Oh?"

Eric glared at his mother. "And thanks to a lack of knowledge sharing on your behalf, I made an ass of myself three different times. If not more. I wasn't prepared for her to be a mother—to twins, no less."

"I see," she said in that slow, maddening way of hers. He could see the wheels turning in her head.

"When's Dad getting home?" he asked in a belated attempt to steer the conversation away from Sofia.

He knew it was Mom sending Christmas cards to the Cortés family, not Dad. Plus Dad's office was cluttered and cozy. They could kick back, drink a beer and watch the Cubs. And not discuss other people's babies.

Elise waved her hand. "He's touring a condo on the Gold Coast that hasn't been on the market for forty years. It's close to the pier you use, it's got amazing views and it's almost three thousand square feet—more than enough room for a family." She smiled prettily. "You should take a look at it. It'll need to be redone, obviously, but..."

His parents were semiretired, but to him, they still seemed as vibrant and active as ever. It helped that Mom had a really good plastic surgeon. She didn't look like she'd had work done but she certainly didn't look like she was in her sixties, either.

However, just because she didn't want to look like a grandmother didn't mean she didn't want grandbabies, because she did.

Oh, yeah—coming here had definitely been a mistake. "Mom, we're not getting into the topic of grandchildren again."

"We're not?" She sounded so innocent that he almost relaxed. Of course that was the exact moment she went for the kill. "Then why does it upset you that Sofia has children?"

"I'm not upset," he snapped. He began to pace. "It just surprised me. I didn't realize..."

"That she'd grown up and moved on with her

life? Yes," his mother said in the caring voice that drove Eric nuts because she really did care. He had friends—Marcus Warren specifically—who had monsters dressed up as parents. Eric knew it was a rare and wonderful thing that he had two parents who not only loved each other but also him. They wanted to see him happy.

"I understand," his mother went on.

"Really, Mom? What do you understand?" He was aware that he was being a jerk—a fact confirmed by the pointed look she gave him. But he couldn't seem to help it.

He found himself thinking about Sofia's twins, Addy and Eddy. They'd been in a tub, their hair crazy and their smiles wide. They loved the water, it was clear. How much fun would they have in the pool? He'd taught Sofia to swim, after all. It would be hilarious to get those two paddling around.

And of course, if the twins were in the water, then Sofia would be with them. Which posed a very important question—bikini or one-piece? He'd love to see her curves in a bathing suit, water sheeting off her body as she pulled herself up the ladder, sun shining off her skin as she lay out under the summer sun to dry out…

He adjusted his trousers and tried to get his mind out of the gutter. It didn't do to fantasize about old friends in his mother's parlor. He should've gone out on his boat. In fact, he'd do that right now. He walked off the Persian rug and jammed his feet into his shoes.

"Things change whether you like it or not," his mother went on. "She changed—and you changed, honey. But you know what I've found?"

"What?" he asked as his mother gracefully rose from her chair and came to stand in front of him, her hands on his shoulders.

"The more things change, the more they stay the same." Even though he'd been nothing but surly to her, she hugged him and Eric hugged her back. "I hope she does well working in the office," Mom said when she leaned back. "She always was a bright, beautiful girl and a true friend to you."

He scowled at his mother. He hated it when she was right. Everything *had* changed. Sofia had grown up into a gorgeous woman who'd loved and lost.

But for all that, Sofia was still bright and beautiful and no matter what she said, they were still friends.

Because some things never changed.

Eric wasn't in the office much. The weather was perfect, so most afternoons he was aboard the *Jennerosity*, speeding away from Chicago and out onto the lake. He could breathe out there, far away from prying eyes and the sounds and smells of the city. He had no trouble being the social playboy people expected one of the "Top Five Billionaire Bachelors of Chicago" to be, but he needed time to recharge.

A few times, he'd been on the verge of asking

Sofia to come with him—hand on the doorknob, question on his lips. But how would that look, giving his brand-new office manager the afternoon off, just to take her boating? Bad, that's how it'd look. So he didn't.

Of course he worked, too. He made a quick trip down to St. Louis to get a look at the property alone. He thought he knew how the city would sell the development's benefits but he liked to check out every potential site unannounced, without anyone else offering their opinions. The property centered around the indoor football stadium that had been recently vacated when St. Louis lost its football team. Without crowds pouring in for weekend home games, whole blocks seemed to be boarded up. Much to Eric's advantage, an attempt to bring in a pro soccer team had recently failed. The city was no doubt growing desperate.

All of which meant he didn't see Sofia for several days. Which was fine. She didn't need him to babysit her. She'd made it plenty clear during their last conversation that the only relationship they could have going forward was a professional one.

That didn't mean he didn't think about her constantly. It took real work to make sure his thoughts stayed away from her body in a bikini and focused on her job performance. Heather reported that Sofia was naturally organized and seemed to be picking up the office systems quickly. "Thank God," she added, tapping her fingers on the desk nervously.

"This final project for school is killing me, but she's taken over enough that I actually got a few hours of sleep last night."

Meryl and Steve had much the same report. Sofia was highly organized, detailed and neat. She asked good questions when she hit a stumbling block. "She's a little quiet," Meryl noted, "but you get the sense she's listening to everything."

"We don't need her to be loud," Steve countered. "That's my job."

Eric rolled his eyes and left his employees to squabble. There was a reason the two of them had their own office removed from everyone else. The Nortons deeply loved each other and they worked well together but their verbal gymnastics could wear on even the mellowest of cube workers.

Eric stood in his office, staring at the lake. Of course Sofia was an organized quick study. He remembered all those times she'd been in the house while he'd had friends over. She'd always hovered on the edge of the conversation until she'd been sure she was welcome to join in. She hadn't been quiet when it'd been just the two of them but for Sofia, at least, two had been company and three was always a crowd.

Were her children like her, quiet and watchful? Or were they handfuls?

He remembered so many things he hadn't thought about in such a long time. The sailboat, the kiss. Teaching her to swim, with her mother watching nervously from the kitchen window. He'd picked out a birthday present for her with his own money, a Barbie with dark hair, just like hers.

But she wasn't that girl, not anymore. Back then, she'd been a kid—and so had he. Now she was a woman and he wanted to get to know her again.

Without being aware of leaving his office, he found himself standing in front of her desk, located on the opposite side of the floor from his.

"Hi," he said, pointedly not staring at her.

Startled, she looked up at him, her dark eyes bright. She looked *amazing*, he realized, his breath catching in his throat. Her color was good and her breath came easily and everything about her radiated calm. In no way, shape or form did she look like she was struggling with the burdens of the job.

But that wasn't what had him unable to tear his gaze away. Somehow, she was even prettier than the last time he'd seen her. Today, she had on a wine-colored jacket over a patterned shirt and her hair was pulled back at the temples, the mass of dark waves spilling down her back. God, how he wanted to peel that jacket and shirt off her and sink his fingers into that silken hair and wind it around his fist so he could angle her head to the side and scrape his teeth over the delicate skin of her—

"Hi," she said, snapping him out of his insanity.

He couldn't respond for a moment as he fought to regain control of his body. Finally, he managed to croak out, "How's it going?"

She notched an eyebrow. "Fine. Haven't seen you for several days." He heard the challenge in her voice. She knew he'd been avoiding her.

But he hadn't been. Not intentionally. "Business waits for no man. I hear you're settling in."

"So far, so good." Her voice was perky and confident, but then she looked down at her desk. "Everyone's been really nice."

He almost heard a...*so far* at the end of that sentence. "But?"

A blush darkened her cheeks. "We're going to St. Louis next week, right?" She worried her lower lip with her teeth.

He almost leaned over to brush his thumb across her lip and soothe the worry away. Somehow, he just managed not to but his hand shook with the effort. She wore a shade of lipstick so deep a red it was almost brown. It looked great on her but God help him, he'd love to mess it up.

Then what she'd said penetrated his thoughts. She was worried about the trip. Was it the thought of traveling—or was it the thought of traveling with him? "Nervous about leaving your babies?" He leaned over and picked up the framed photo she'd put on her desk. This was a formal shot and, if he had to guess, he'd say it was for the twins' one-year birthday.

God, they were cute. Eddy, dressed in a tiny tie that was hilarious on him, was standing with his hands on a small stool. Addy, wearing a dress that almost swallowed her whole and bows on itty-bitty ponytails, sat on a blanket next to the stool. Both kids were grinning wildly and Addy was clapping. They looked…perfect. Something in his chest tightened as he stared at the picture.

He said a silent prayer for their father. What a damn shame that the man hadn't lived long enough to love his perfect family. If Eric had a wife like Sofia and kids like these babies, he wouldn't have done anything stupid like die. He'd spend the rest of his life making sure this family was happy and whole. He'd give them every opportunity he'd ever had and more.

His mind spun out a—well, a fantasy. Working with Sofia, then going home with her at the end of the day, doing all those things he'd watched Marcus do with his wife and son—messy dinners and playing in the park. Then, when the kids went to bed at night, Eric would pull Sofia into his arms and into bed, where he'd spend the better part of the night—and the next morning—getting lost in the pleasures of her body.

It was almost perfect, that little fantasy of his. But he couldn't just step into Sofia's life like that. He did not sleep with employees. Hell, he shouldn't even be fantasizing about them.

Belatedly, he realized Sofia hadn't answered his question. He glanced up and caught her staring at him staring at her picture. Trying to act casual, he set it back on the desk. "I'd miss them, too," he admitted, touching the frame with his finger. "How are they doing with you being at work?"

"It's been a little rough," she said quietly, as if she were afraid someone might overhear her admit to a weakness. She quickly added, "But it's not impacting my ability to do the job, Mr. Jenner."

It should have been the thing he wanted to hear. Yes, he wanted his employees happy, but only because he wanted them to do their jobs to the best of their abilities.

So why did her words bother him so much?

He must have scowled because her eyes widened in what looked like alarm.

"Then what's bothering you?" he asked.

She didn't answer for a moment. Instead, her gaze lingered on his face before drifting down to his shoulders and the rest of his body.

Eric liked to think he wasn't a stupid man. He liked women on principle. He'd been enjoying them in one capacity or another since he'd gone away to school.

So he didn't think he was misinterpreting the way Sofia took in his body or the way the color on her cheeks deepened as her gaze met his again.

Interest. Attraction, even. Sofia looked at him as if he was a man she might just like to take a weekend trip with. And his body responded in a primal way. He heard his voice deepen when he said, "You can tell me, Sofia. You know that."

Her gaze jerked up to meet his. Her eyes were

dark with desire and when she ran her tongue over her bottom lip, he went painfully hard. His body tilted toward hers of its own volition.

She glanced away, breaking the spell. "I was looking at the itinerary and it says we're having dinner with the lieutenant governor and a cocktail party with the mayor? I don't know what to wear…"

Ah, this was a problem he understood. "Is that all?"

"No," she said quietly. Her face turned bright red. "I mean, that's the only thing that I'm concerned I won't be prepared for. For the trip. The kids will be fine. We're only going to be gone two nights, right?"

"Right. We'll leave Friday morning and be back Sunday evening."

He knew what he needed to do. He'd have to give up his afternoon on the water but for some irrational reason, he found himself looking forward to it. Because this was one way to get her out of those stuffy jackets.

"Tell you what," he began. "We'll take the afternoon off and get you something to wear."

Limos, while practically a requirement for billionaires, were damned inconvenient to get around in downtown Chicago. Eric vastly preferred his Ferrari F60—one of only ten made—and he preferred driving himself.

Which meant Sofia was sitting next to him, clutching the door handle as if her life depended on it as he weaved through traffic on his way to Barneys. Her scent filled the car, warm and light. She smelled so good, like cookies fresh out of the oven. That had to be why he wanted to press his lips against the base of her neck and take a little bite.

"Macy's is fine. Even Nordstrom," she said for the sixth time.

To Eric's ears, she sounded almost desperate about it. Which was enough to keep him focused on the task at hand. Barely. "Come on, Sofia. I'm not exactly leading you to the gallows here. It's just a department store." They came to a screeching halt at a stoplight and he glanced over at her.

No, she wasn't happy. He had to be careful that he didn't accidentally push her too far. A cocktail dress was no reason to have a panic attack, in his opinion.

She snorted. "Eric," she began and he secretly thrilled to hear her use his name again. It bothered him more than he'd realized that she'd called him Mr. Jenner. "Look. I can't afford anything in this store, okay?"

Yeah, but he was buying. "Don't worry about it."

The light turned green but, in true Chicago fashion, he had to wait for another four cars to blow through the red before he could go.

"No," she said, sounding stronger. "We're not ten anymore. And don't you dare turn into your mother, buying me frilly dresses that I'll never be able to wear again."

"First off, how dare you?" he said in mock outrage and she laughed. He grinned wildly at her. This was how he liked her—not cautious or worried, but ready and willing to give him hell. "I'm nothing like my mother, I'll have you know. Any dress I buy you won't be frilly." Even as he said it, his mind began to leap ahead. Sofia had the kind of body that called out for something slinky that cut close to her body, with a deep V in front so he could properly appreciate her…assets.

"You can't buy me clothes, Eric," she said in a quiet voice. "Would you buy Meryl clothes? Or Steve, for that matter?"

He scowled at a car that cut in front of him. "No, but they already know what's expected. Besides, if you think I'm going to let you walk into a situation where you're unprepared, you don't know me as well as you think you do."

But she was right. He wouldn't buy clothes for anyone else, wouldn't give anyone else the afternoon off and take them shopping. Just her.

He cleared his throat as the car came to a screeching halt outside Barneys. The valet was at Eric's door in an instant. "Mr. Jenner, good to see you again," the man said.

"Norman," Eric replied, handing over his keys. "Extra gentle with her, okay?" From the passenger seat, Sofia snorted.

He crossed around the front of the vehicle and opened Sofia's door. "It won't be that bad," he promised, holding out his hand to her. "It might even be fun."

Because, oddly, he was having fun. Sofia shot him a dirty look, which made him want to laugh. The few times he'd taken a woman shopping, they'd always simpered and smiled and were so effusive with gratitude that it had seemed less...real, somehow.

He didn't want things to be like that with Sofia. He was aware of her in a fundamental way that didn't make a lot of sense. He knew what she liked and, more than that, he knew what she needed.

Hell, he knew what he needed—but he was trying to be a better person. In the months since his ex had bailed on their wedding, he'd re-sowed a lot of his wild oats. But he wasn't a randy kid anymore and meaningless sex was just that—meaningless. He didn't want to chase a sexual relationship with Sofia if...

Well, if it didn't mean anything. Because even if this relationship never became sexual, Sofia meant something to him. More than an office manager, anyway. Much more.

Then she put her hand in his and the world stopped spinning. He didn't hear the noise of the streets or feel the heat of the summer sun on the back of his neck. He didn't see anything but her as she raised her gaze to his. All he saw was Sofia, her hand warm and light in his. Skin to skin, he swore he felt something pass between them. Something that maybe had tugged at his awareness when he'd touched her back through her jacket during her interview. Something that couldn't be ignored now.

"Come on," he said gruffly, pulling her to her feet and tucking her hand in the crook of his elbow. He didn't trust himself to say anything else.

Six

Sofia stared up at Eric in shock. What was happening? Really? Eric had been avoiding her since she'd scolded him—and she couldn't blame him. No one wanted to hang out with a harpy. But suddenly he'd appeared in front of her desk and not only asked thoughtful questions about her twins, but seemed genuinely interested in the answers. And then, when she broke her own rule about telling him she wasn't prepared for her job? He took her shopping.

At best, she might have expected him to send her out to Macy's with Heather, who no doubt knew exactly what kind of dress an office manager should wear to a cocktail party with the mayor of a midsize Midwestern city.

But that wasn't what was happening. Eric was

going to take her shopping himself. At Barneys, of all places. Even with her newly generous salary, Sofia couldn't afford to so much as walk through the doors here.

Well. This was a fine mess. She should refuse, absolutely. Except…

Except he really seemed to care about how her babies were doing now that she was back at work full-time. And sometimes, when he looked at her… she swore he was looking at her with new eyes. And she had nothing to wear and didn't want to show up at a semiformal event representing the company in the wrong kind of dress.

No, that wasn't the whole truth. It wasn't just that she didn't want to feel out of place at a fancy party. She didn't want to feel out of place when Eric looked at her.

She knew she didn't belong in his world. He was so far above her in terms of looks and money and power… That she was even considering this was a clear indication of how nuts she was. But was it wrong if, at least for a weekend, she wanted to pretend that she fit into his glamorous life? That they were equals?

That she was good enough for him?

It'd been so long since she'd felt attractive. Pregnancy had done a number on her self-esteem and then, after David's death, she hadn't exactly kept up her appearance. Who cared about under-eye concealer when she could barely force herself out of bed every morning? It'd only been in the last six months—coincidentally, about the same time the twins started sleeping through the night—that she'd been able to get past the fog and start putting herself on the list of people to take care of.

How was she supposed to do *this* with *Eric*? When he looked at her with his intense eyes, it made her want to do stupid, stupid things—like let him lavish her with the finest dresses money could buy. Like hope that he'd remove those fine dresses from her body and pull her into his arms and…

She cleared her throat, trying to get her pulse to stay at a steady rhythm. What was she going to do?

Apparently, she was going to let Eric buy her clothes. It was wildly inappropriate and completely beyond the normal boundaries of common sense. God only knew what the gossip at the office would be tomorrow or—worse—after the St. Louis trip.

But did she have a choice? She didn't even have a proper suit that fit anymore. She'd been making do with the cutest separates she could find. She'd gotten her first paycheck—with a number that was still stunning to her—but she hadn't had time to go buy some work clothes. She couldn't sacrifice any more time away from her babies for something as superficial as trousers.

Except for this damned cocktail party, that was. And heavens help her, she wanted to look good for him.

Her chest began to tighten in panic but she pushed

back and made sure to count to four as she breathed in and then out.

"Mr. Jenner," a polished woman who might have been in her forties or her sixties said, coming forward to meet them. "How lovely to see you back at Barneys again."

"Clarice," Eric said, and Sofia heard a particular tone to his voice that he didn't use with her. Imperious, she might have called it. "This is Ms. Bingham."

Clarice turned her sharp gaze to Sofia. "Yes," she said, as if she'd just figured out that Sofia didn't belong here. "Ms. Bingham, if you'd come this way? I have some options already pulled, but of course I want to take your opinions under consideration."

"Wait—I thought…" Sofia looked dumbly at Eric. She'd assumed he'd be an active part of this. Was she wrong? She'd been nervous about him offering his opinion on each outfit. So how was the realization that he wouldn't somehow even *worse*?

His face softened with a smile and she almost sighed in relief. She didn't like him all imperious. Then he took her by the arm and led her a little away from Clarice, who immediately made it her business to focus anywhere but on them. "Surprise me," he said as he slid his hand down and pressed her palm against his. A silky warmth flowed between them.

Her body tightened with want because oh, how she wanted to surprise him. But want had nothing to do with this. It couldn't. "Eric, we can't do this," she murmured—which was true and also did nothing to explain why she couldn't seem to pull her hand away from his.

"Don't you dare accuse me of turning into my mother again," he said as his thumb charted a steady course along the base of hers.

"Your mother would never—" She barely managed to get her mouth shut before something really inappropriate, like "look at me like she wants to undress me," came tumbling out. "Bring me here," she finished weakly.

"Shows what you know." His grin faded and somehow, he got even closer to her. "I want to do this for you, Sofia. I want you to walk into that cocktail party looking beautiful and feeling like you've got the world at your feet because you are and you do. I can see it. I want everyone else—including you—to see it, too." His fingers laced with hers, pulling her in. She was powerless to let go of him. "What I don't want is for you to feel like you've lost control. If you start to panic, call me immediately, okay?" When she didn't answer right away, he said, "Let me take care of you," in an even softer voice.

It simply wasn't fair of him to make her fall a little in love with him in the middle of a damned upscale department store. But that's what happened. Eric Jenner was a sinfully rich, sinfully handsome bachelor and for some inexplicable reason, he cared about her. He understood her panic attacks. He gave her a chance. He made her smile. He made things better. How could she *not* fall for him? "All right." It came out husky and low and not at all like her normal voice. But then, there wasn't exactly anything normal about any of this.

His eyes darkened as his gaze dropped to her lips and without conscious choice, she licked them under his watchful eye. He inhaled sharply and then abruptly he stepped away from her, dropping her hand like it was hot. "I'll…" He cleared his throat and tried again. "I'll be in the menswear department."

And with that parting shot, he turned on his heel and strode off. All Sofia could do was watch him go. Her hand was still warm from where they'd been skin to skin and she had to fight the ridiculous urge to run after him.

Clarice appeared at her elbow. "Are you ready?" she asked, her voice crisp.

It took real effort to tear her gaze away from where Eric's back was disappearing down the stairs. Once again, he was putting a great deal of faith in her.

If he wanted to be surprised, then that's what she'd give him.

"I think so."

But when they made it back to a private fitting room, there were more than just a few cocktail dresses waiting. There were racks and racks of clothing, including business suits and shoes and even underwear. "What is all this?" Sofia asked, pressing her hand to her chest in alarm.

"When Mr. Jenner and I spoke on the phone, he made it clear that you would need to be outfitted for a cocktail party, business meetings and travel," Clarice said, smiling in a way that was probably supposed to be reassuring. "Isn't that what you two discussed?"

"Um…" He hadn't said anything about suits or traveling clothes. This was supposed to be a dress. One dress. Not an entire wardrobe. "How many outfits are we talking about here?"

Clarice didn't hesitate. "Two business suits, two evening outfits and two traveling outfits. Mr. Jenner made it clear that you were to be outfitted and accessorized from head to toe."

Sofia's heart began to hammer in her chest. This was too much. What part of six damned outfits that he hadn't even discussed with her was making sure she didn't feel like she was losing control?

She opened her mouth to refuse it all—the carte blanche, the outfits, Clarice's knowledgeable assistance—and then she remembered what Eric had said as he'd held her hand and leaned toward her. He wanted to do this for her because he knew she was beautiful and he wanted her to believe it, too.

She closed her eyes and made sure she was still breathing. Oh, this was dangerous, that she was even considering this. She didn't just want to surprise him when she walked into that cocktail party and she didn't just want to look like she fit.

She wanted to feel pretty again.

She wanted to make Eric's brain stop functioning.
"Can you make me look great? Like, really great?"

Clarice's eyes lit up. "It would be my pleasure."

Seven

Sofia was a mess of nerves. She hadn't been able to eat breakfast and hadn't slept more than twenty or thirty minutes at a time last night. For once, it had nothing to do with the twins teething.

Her luggage, packed with five different outfits and three pairs of shoes for a three-day trip, stood by the front door, waiting. Eric was going to pick her up sometime in the next fifteen minutes and drive her to the airport. From there, he, Sofia and the Nortons would fly in Eric's private jet to St. Louis.

She was doing this. She was going away for a weekend with Eric. Business trip be damned. She had sexy lingerie in her bag, far too beautiful to keep hidden underneath clothes.

No, no—she wasn't nervous about that. Eric

wasn't going to see her panties. She was just…nervous about flying. She'd been on an airplane exactly twice in her life, flying to and from Cancún for her honeymoon with David. She hadn't liked it then, and that had been a big plane. Eric's jet wasn't much more than a puddle jumper.

In fact, the only thing keeping her from a full-on panic attack was the fact that she was being mobbed by adorable babies.

"Are you going to miss me when I'm gone?" she asked, sitting on the floor with both Addy and Eddy on her lap. Eddy's lip began to tremble. "I'll come back," she promised. "I always come back, don't I? You'll have a lot of fun with Abuelita and Abuelito. Story time at the library, a trip to the park—"

"Pak!" Eddy yelled, flopping off her lap and toddling over to where his shoes were.

Sofia laughed. The boy would sell his sister for a swing set. "Later," she said. "When Miss Rita gets here, you can go to the park." Rita was a new addition to their routine, a young woman who reminded Sofia of what Rosa must've been like twenty or thirty years ago. Rita was a first-generation Mexican American, taking night classes, already working one part-time job and now helping out with the twins in the mornings.

Watching Rosa Cortés with Rita was a little like watching Mrs. Jenner buy dresses for Sofia when she had been a girl. Mom went out of her way to make extra food that Rita could take home because she wouldn't have time to get anything before class. Mom often had a sweater or a dress that she'd bought because she'd thought it would fit, but when she got it home it didn't—and it just happened to be in Rita's size.

Sofia was just glad Mom liked Rita and seemed to embrace her help with the twins. Sofia worried less about her parents now that there was backup.

That didn't make it any easier to leave her babies, though. Addy snuggled into Sofia's lap, her thumb in her mouth. Sofia stroked her daughter's hair, savoring this moment of closeness. God, she was going to miss them. But she wasn't going to cry. She swallowed hard a few times as she breathed in Addy's sweet baby smell. No crying allowed.

But was it wrong she was excited about this weekend trip? She was going to have a hotel room all to herself at the Chase Park Plaza, with room service and no one to wake her up in the middle of the night. She wouldn't have to cook or clean. She had two new dresses that made her feel beautiful and the company of a man who made her want more than she could even dream about.

She had no right to dream of him, but that hadn't stopped her from wondering if he'd wear a tux to this party. Or how he'd look if she reached up and tugged on that bow tie, unraveling the ends and pulling him toward her and—

The doorbell rang and Addy launched herself off Sofia's lap. She and Eddy ran to the door.

"That's the driver, Mom," Sofia called to her mother in the kitchen, her stomach doing a little flutter. She gathered the black pashmina wrap Clarice had insisted pulled the whole look together and her purse. That, at least, was still hers. She couldn't bring herself to let the accessorizing go so far as to include handbags. She knew exactly how expensive those things could be.

It was ridiculous that he was coming for her. He could've saved himself a lot of time if they'd met at the office.

But no. And he didn't even send a separate car. Instead, his driver was picking her up, even though it was way out of the way to drive from the Gold Coast where Eric lived down to the Pilsen neighborhood where she lived with her parents.

The Nortons lived close to the Chicago Executive Airport, where Eric kept his plane—which was on the far northern side of the city. So they'd meet them there. Which meant it would just be Eric and Sofia in the car. In the back seat. Hidden from the rest of the world.

Not that it mattered, because it didn't. This was a work-related trip. The brand-new clothes she was wearing were work clothes—although Sofia had not yet figured out in what alternative universe a silk georgette blouse and cropped white trousers constituted a "traveling outfit." In her world, white pants were a disaster waiting to happen. But she was wearing them anyway. The same went for the cocktail dresses. The outfits had nothing to do with the way Eric had held her hand in the store or told her to let him take care of her. Not a damned thing.

She might engage in some gentle flirting because that seemed unavoidable. But Eric flirted with everyone, so that was fine. Safe, even. As long as they kept it at flirting. No undressing, no lingerie.

The doorbell rang again. Sofia took hold of Addy as Mom hurried out of the kitchen to scoop up Eddy.

Sofia opened the door, saying, "My bag is—"

The man standing in the doorway was not the driver. Eric Jenner himself stood there, looking sinfully handsome in a brightly colored button-up shirt with a linen blazer over it. Her mouth fell open and all she could do was stare at him. His hair had more of a wave than normal and he looked so damn good she could feel her resolve crumbling like a cookie in a toddler's hands—and they hadn't even made it to the car yet.

She was going away with him for the weekend. And he wanted to take care of her.

Oh, God.

"Sofia," Eric began, but then his gaze was drawn to Addy, who'd curled against Sofia's shoulder. "Good heavens," he went on, sounding almost severe about it. "These children are even cuter in person than they are in pictures. I didn't think that was physically possible."

"Mr. Eric!" Mom said, struggling to hold on to Eddy. "Oh—we weren't expecting you! Oh!" she said again, her hand flying to her chest as she looked him over. "My, you've grown up so much!"

Eric took that as an invitation. He stepped inside and closed the door behind him. Then, before Sofia's eyes, he bowed. Bowed! "Mrs. Cortés, you haven't changed a bit. You are as lovely as I remember."

Mom blushed—which only made Sofia stare even more. When was the last time her mother had blushed? "Mr. Eric, we can't thank you enough for everything—"

Eric waved her off. "Sofia's doing a great job, just like I knew she would." Then he leaned forward and said, "May I?" Without waiting for an answer, he plucked Eddy from her mother's arms. "You must be Eduardo. I can tell—you're a very serious young man." As he said it, he tickled Eddy's tummy.

Eddy squealed with delight and kept right on squealing as Eric lifted the boy over his head a few times, saying, "Oh, yes—very serious indeed."

That got Addy's attention. Although she didn't fling herself at Eric, she sat up. She didn't have to wait long. Eric tucked Eddy into the crook of one arm and reached out for Addy. "Hello, Miss Adelina. Aren't you a good girl?"

"It's all right," Sofia reassured her and then Addy was lifted from her arms and cradled against Eric's chest.

"There we are," Eric said reassuringly, bouncing both children a little bit. Eddy seemed thrilled beyond words, but Addy was holding herself a little apart from him, still unsure about this strange man who'd just walked into their lives.

Next to her, Mom sighed—a noise that was part happiness, part relief and part...longing, maybe? Sofia could sympathize. The sight of her children in Eric's arms—if possible, this was even less fair than him tenderly telling her that he wanted her to feel as beautiful as she was.

Because he was holding her children, making silly sounds and getting Addy to smile while Eddy tried to copy his sounds, with varying degrees of success.

Eric was perfect.

"Oh, Mr. Eric—I have something for you," Mom said, hurrying off to the kitchen.

And leaving them alone. "Hi," he said over the heads of the twins. His eyes warmed as he looked her over. "It's good to see you."

Oh, Lord—the only thing worse than flirting right now was sincere compliments because there was no defense against sincerity. "Hi," she said back.

What was she supposed to say here? Because it simply wasn't fair how perfect he was. The least the universe could do would be to make him not like children. If he showed indifference or even open dislike of the twins, it would be so much easier to keep her attraction to him under control.

But no. He had to be perfect in every way. He was going to make her fall in love with him and it was going to break her heart.

"Hey, can you take a picture? I'll send it to my mom," he said. "Can we smile, kiddos?"

By the time she got the camera app open, they were all laughing. No, this wasn't fair at all. "Babies!" she said enthusiastically, which got both twins to focus on her. Eric looked up and grinned and she snapped several shots.

Then Eddy squirmed out of his arms and Sofia had to hide her smile at Eric trying to juggle the twins. But he didn't drop either toddler, so that counted for something. "What is it, big guy?"

Chattering excitedly, Eddy made his way over to the coloring table. "He wants to show you his drawings. Which means that, in about ten seconds, Addy will want to show you *her* drawings, too."

"A little friendly sibling rivalry?"

"You have no idea."

"Sofia?" Mom poked her head out of the kitchen. "Can you give me a hand before you leave?"

Sofia frowned at her mother. Normally the woman refused any and all offers of help. But Mom gave her *the look* and Sofia had no choice but to say to Eric, "Will you be all right for a minute?"

"Go on," he said, shooting her a grin that made her cheeks heat.

Mom had a small pile of food assembled on the counter. "Mom, what are you doing?"

"Mr. Eric—he always loved Jarritos. I think I have another bottle of the *fresa* somewhere..." she said to herself, digging around one of the cabinets.

"Ah, here it is." She pulled out the bottle of the red drink.

Strawberry had always been Sofia's favorite, too. "Did you call me in here just to help you find some soda?" Her heart began to pound faster, but it didn't feel like a panic attack waiting to happen.

"No, *cariño.*" Her mom set the soda down by the other snacks—all Mexican brands. Bags of corn chips and pastries. The kind of snacks she'd loved growing up. She remembered how Eric had always treated Takis chips like a rare and special treat.

"I want you to promise me something," Mom said, her brow knit with worry.

What was this all about? It wasn't like her mother to be overly dramatic. "Okay, what?"

"I want you to have some fun this weekend." She said it in such a hushed, serious tone—like she was confessing to a sin.

"Fun?" Sofia shook her head from side to side, wondering when the world stopped making sense. Fun had always been low on her mother's priority list. "Mom, this is a business trip. We'll be working."

Her mother clucked and patted Sofia on the cheek and just like that, Sofia felt like she was seven again. "*Ayi*, it is—but this is the first time since David died that you've…" Her voice trailed off.

Sofia was suddenly terrified of what her mother might say. Because what it sounded like Mom was saying was that it might be a good idea if Sofia considered sleeping with her boss on a weekend getaway and that couldn't possibly be true. Especially not when Sofia had been daydreaming about doing just that.

"There's nothing going on here. We're just old friends who happen to work together now."

Her mother gave her another look, one that had Sofia's mouth snapping shut on any other protest. "It's been almost a year and a half. You need to move on with your life."

Sofia stared in disbelief, but Rosa Cortés didn't so much as blink. "I am moving on. I got a new job and some new clothes." Clothes that Eric had paid for. "There's nothing else I need from him." It didn't matter how much that might be a lie—she was sticking to it.

"Nothing?" Mom clucked again and dug out a bag to put the snacks in. "He grew up. So handsome. And thoughtful, to come get you himself." She sighed again and Sofia swore she could see stars in her mother's eyes. "The twins love him. You can just tell."

She could. Even Addy had warmed up to him in record time. "Mom…"

Because this was not the beginning of a new story. This was not a happily-ever after in the making. And if Sofia allowed herself to buy into that delusion—that a hot, rich, thoughtful billionaire who cared for her and the children would somehow give her a perfect family and a storybook life—no. He was so far out of her league that she knew she'd fall if she tried to climb to his level. And she couldn't fall again. She wouldn't survive the bounce this time.

"It's just that you've been through so much—you deserve a little fun, don't you?" Mom nodded to herself as she bagged up the snacks. "It's time for you to smile again."

"I smile. I smile all the time." It was hard not to smile and laugh when Addy and Eddy were being adorable—or even when they were getting into trouble.

But even as she thought that, Sofia knew she was being deliberately obtuse because that's not what Mom was talking about and they both knew it.

Sorrow pulled at the corners of Mom's mouth. "Ah, you smile for your children. You even smile for me and your father, as if you think we can't see how you're hiding behind it. But, *cariño*, when was the last time you smiled for *yourself*?" With that parting shot, Mom carried the overflowing bag of snacks and sodas out to Eric.

Sofia stood there, struggling to breathe. Mom was wrong. That's all there was to it. She smiled. She was moving on and living her life. She…

Sofia dropped her head into her hands. She didn't get enough sleep and every day was a new battle to be waged against crushing depression and anxiety. Her entire life had become faking it until she made it. Apparently, she wasn't faking it well enough to fool her own mother.

And what, exactly, was that woman encouraging

her to do? Seduce Eric? Have an affair with her boss? It didn't make any sense. Although she had liked David and approved of the marriage, Rosa Cortés had been horrified when Sofia and David had moved in together before the wedding. Mom was a very traditional woman. She would never do anything as risqué as condone an affair.

But the moment the thoughts of seduction and Eric ran headlong into each other in Sofia's head, her mind oh-so-helpfully filled in the blanks. A big soft bed in a hotel room, Eric looking at her with desire in his eyes as she slipped the buttons free on his shirt and he slid down the zipper on her dress. Would he pounce on her, all masculine strength and raw lust? Or would it be a slow seduction, one that left her shaking and begging for release?

God, she missed sex.

"Wow—Takis? I haven't had these in years!" she heard Eric say. Sofia swung around to see him surge to his feet as Mom held out the snacks. "I can't believe you remembered how much I liked these!" He rummaged through the bag. "And Conchas? Oh, man—these are always such a special treat! Sofia always shared these."

Sofia watched as her mom ducked her head, another girlish blush on her cheeks. "We always brought extra for you. But not too much—we didn't want to make your mother mad."

"As long as we didn't get orange fingerprints on

her office furniture…" They laughed, as if the passage of years had never happened.

Have fun. Maybe Sofia was reading too much into this.

It wasn't like she could just decide not to be anxious. It didn't work that way. But she could make a conscious choice to enjoy herself this weekend. She could continue to fake it until she made it because even if she'd still be forcing herself to smile, she might eventually make it to having a good time. To enjoying her time with Eric. Even if that just meant sharing a bag of fried corn chips.

Or even if it meant something…more.

God, it'd be so good to smile again. To be happy again. At least now, she could almost see happiness from where she stood. It wasn't a star hung too high in the sky that she'd never be able to reach, like it'd been in the first terrible months after David's death.

She'd never forget her husband—she didn't want to—but maybe it wasn't such a bad thing that Eric reminded her she'd been a happy, whole person before her marriage and she might be one again.

As she watched, Eric pulled Mom into an impulsive hug. "It's been so great to see you again, Mrs. Cortés. My parents always love to hear from you."

"Give my best to your mother." Just then, Eric's watch beeped. "Oh, you must go. You'll be late! I wouldn't want you to miss your flight."

Eric laughed. "Don't worry. They won't leave without me."

Eddy toddled over to him, holding up a sheet of paper. Eric bent down. "This is really nice, big guy. Did you make this for me?"

Eddy grinned widely and nodded. Not to be outdone, here came Addy, also brandishing a sheet of paper. "Oh, this is lovely," Eric said so seriously that Sofia couldn't help but laugh. "Can you write your name on it for me?"

Addy hurried to the table and then slashed a line in bright pink across the bottom.

"That's my girl," Eric said and another part of Sofia melted.

He would be *so* easy to fall for. She could fight against the fact that he was gorgeous and the fact that he had more money than most of the rest of the city put together. She could even work around the way he treated her with kindness. But this?

Because right now, he wasn't some unreachable fantasy. Right now, he was joking with her mother, making her babies smile—all while waiting to whisk her away for the weekend. She could almost pretend he fit in her world.

She only hoped she could pretend she fit in his. Just for a few days. Just to have a little fun.

Eddy signed his art, too—he chose a red crayon for his signature scribble. "I will treasure these always, guys," Eric said, folding the two sheets of paper and tucking them into an inside pocket. "I'll come back and see you again, okay? And maybe your mom will bring you out on the boat. We'll go swimming and everything."

Swimming didn't mean much to the twins—but *boat*? "Now you've done it," she told him as she came out of the kitchen, her resolve set. They were going to have a lovely weekend and that was final.

Sofia leaned down to give each of the twins another kiss on the head. "Be good," she told them. "I'll see you in a few days. Love you."

Eric put his hand in the small of Sofia's back. "Longer goodbyes only make it harder," he said, his voice low in her ear.

He guided her through the door and down the front steps, where a long black car was waiting. It wasn't quite a limousine, but it was close.

She looked back over her shoulder to see Mom holding the twins at the window, everyone waving. Sofia had to blink hard as she waved back and then Eric had the door open for her and she climbed into his luxury car.

He sat next to her and put the bag of snacks between them. "Ready to have some fun?"

She picked up one of the snacks. *Fun*. Nothing more and by God, nothing less. "Let's go wild."

Eight

Normally, Eric enjoyed everything about traveling to a site at the beginning of a new project. Of course he enjoyed making more money. Who didn't? But he actually loved buying a piece of property, whether it was vacant or the buildings were dilapidated or whatever, and seeing the possibilities. He loved choosing the best option from those possibilities and making it a reality. He was good at it, too. Every development was more successful than the last. Sometimes it seemed like there wasn't anything Eric couldn't turn to gold.

He glanced at the woman sitting across from him. She looked amazing today—but his awareness of her went deeper than just how her backside had looked in those white pants when she'd gotten into the car.

So many possibilities.

It didn't make any sense, how glad he was to see her. He'd gone decades without Sofia in his life and suddenly, he was waking up early, thinking of ways he could make her laugh—or make her eyes deepen with desire, make her tongue flick over her lips in anticipation…

"Should I send that picture to you or your mother?" Sofia asked.

He jerked his gaze away from her lips. "Me." Because he wanted to hold on to that memory of Sofia's children in his arms, of Eddy's easy laughter, of Addy's slow but sweet smile.

He hadn't lied—those kids were even cuter in person. Eddy was outgoing and Addy was reserved, but they were two sides of the same coin. They weren't identical, in either their appearance or temperament, but they did little things together that tugged at his heartstrings, like tilting their heads the same way and smiling the same smile at the same time. They matched each other perfectly in every way.

He touched his jacket, right over where he'd tucked their drawings in his inside pocket. When he thought of those babies, all he saw was possibilities.

His reaction didn't make any sense, but he wanted to be there for them.

"There," Sofia said, seconds before his phone chimed. "You like strawberry best, right? I suppose it's not a great idea to load up on junk food before we get on the plane, though…" She fished out a bright red Jarritos soda from the overflowing bag Mrs. Cortés had packed.

"At least we won't starve to death anytime soon," he joked, twisting the cap off the soda. "I haven't had one of these in years." He took a long drink. And then immediately started coughing as the sugar hit his tongue like a tidal wave. "Was it always this sweet?" he choked out, his eyes watering.

Sofia laughed. He could see a little of the tension fading from around her eyes. "Yes, it was. You really haven't had one since we were kids?"

He shook his head and took a much smaller sip of the soda. All he could taste was sugar. It wasn't so much strawberry flavored, but damn if it didn't taste like his childhood and all the fun he used to have with Sofia. "I know you may find this hard to believe, but I don't exactly wander the aisles of grocery stores. I have a personal chef and I dine out a lot."

Her lips twisted into something that might've been a smile. Yes, he knew she didn't have personal chefs, but he didn't want to do a side-by-side comparison of their lifestyles.

"That's true, I suppose," she said.

"Hey, none of that." He held out his soda for her to taste. Mrs. Cortés had packed several bottles but he was possessed with the sudden urge to share with Sofia. They always had shared, back when they'd been kids, hiding from his mom's nutritionally conscious eyes. "We're going to have a good time this weekend and that's final. I don't know if I told you this yet, but you look very nice today."

She hesitated and then took the bottle from him. "Thank you. I can't take any credit for this outfit— or anything else. It's all Clarice."

"She may have picked it out," he said, his gaze drawn to the smooth expanse of her creamy skin revealed by the low-cut blouse, "but you're making it look good."

Sofia's cheeks shot bright pink and for a second, he thought she was going to scold him. Instead, she lifted the bottle and placed it against her lips.

Suddenly, Eric couldn't do anything but watch her throat move as she swallowed. When she handed the bottle back to him, her tongue traced the path around her lips, capturing every drop of sweetness.

He went hard in a heartbeat and it only got worse when she looked up at him through her lashes. So many possibilities. How would she look, her hair un- done and her lips swollen from kisses? Would she taste sweet or would she taste more complex, like a fine wine?

He shook back to himself. This was Sofia, for crying out loud. He had to stop thinking about kiss- ing her at random times. About kissing her at all. Or about what she'd look like in a cocktail dress. Or even out of a cocktail dress.

Unfortunately, his thoughts went right back to her children. He dug out his phone and opened the picture and froze. Eddy was clapping, Addy was smiling and as for him?

He looked happy. Happier than he could ever remember looking.

This was bad. No, that wasn't true. *Bad* was wanting to strip her down to nothing and spending a long evening in a private hotel suite showing her how much better he'd gotten at kissing since he'd been a kid. He wanted to do bad, bad things to her. Repeatedly. Over the course of a long weekend.

Her babies weren't bad, because he now knew these twins and might very well keep on knowing them. He could visit them again or have Sofia bring them out on the boat. Hell, he could invite them to his parents' house because his mother would go crazy for these babies. He didn't have to cling to this one photo as if that was all he was going to get.

But it was worse, too—because how was he supposed to spend time with those babies and not want more? He could already see it all—the way they'd scream in delight as the boat roared across the lake. How much fun they'd have in the pool, splashing everywhere.

How was he supposed to spend time with *Sofia* and not think of stripping her down and covering her body with his every other second? How was he supposed to hold himself back from cupping her cheek in his palm, feeling the soft warmth of her skin against his?

He shifted in his seat. What was his problem? He

was *not* thinking about seducing Sofia, damn it. And he couldn't be anything more to her children than an old family friend, either. As much as he cared for Sofia and her children, it wasn't like he could just snap his fingers and have a ready-made family come running to his side.

It was one thing to give Sofia a good salary to support her children—but another thing to think he could overcome the loss of her husband and the babies' father. All the money and power in the world couldn't replace David Bingham.

A happy ending for Sofia was one more thing he couldn't buy.

But if he could, he would. Because he did care for Sofia and he could very easily care for her children.

So many possibilities.

She opened a bag of Takis chips and held it out to him. "Thank you for being nice to the kids."

He snorted and took a chip. "You make it sound like I was forcing myself to endure their company and that couldn't be further from the truth. I'm only sorry we couldn't hang out more. And," he went on, cutting her off before she could argue with him, "I was serious about coming out on the boat. I'll get life preservers for them. Or maybe those little wet suits with the built-in floaties? Marcus had one for his son."

That set off another round of thoughts. Marcus had married his executive assistant—Liberty Reese, who Eric had tried to poach for his own office.

How had that worked out for the Warrens? They still ran Warren Capital together. They'd adopted a little baby and somehow made a family out of almost thin air.

He shook his head. Those were questions best left for later. "While it's a little cooler out toward the middle of the lake, the water's a lot cleaner," he went on. "The back of my boat opens out almost level with the water, so there wouldn't be a big jump for them. I think they'd love it." Then he popped the chip into his mouth.

And coughed again as his tongue caught on fire. "Were these always *this* spicy?" he spluttered, grabbing the soda and downing the rest of it in seconds. His eyes began to water as sweat popped out on his forehead.

Sofia laughed at him. "No, actually," she said, studying the bag. "These are a newer flavor. Too hot?"

"I wasn't prepared, that's all." But even as he said it, he swore he could see smoke curling out of his mouth. "I might never be prepared. Let's not take these out on the boat. I'd never forgive myself if one of the kids ate one by accident."

Her eyes narrowed as she studied him—although it was hard to look severe when eating corn chips. She didn't even seem to break a sweat eating those hellfire chips. "You're really serious? About the boat?"

"Sofia, when have I ever not been serious?"

She fought against a smile, he could tell. Her mouth twisted before she lost the battle and grinned at him. "Gosh," she said, taking a pastry from the bag. "I can't think of a time where you were never *not* serious."

He liked that smile on her. He didn't want to see worry crowding the corners of her eyes, drawing her full lips into a tight line. "Are you going to be okay this weekend?"

She looked out the window. "I think so. Yes. This is a whole different world for me, Eric. Private jets and expensive clothes and chauffeured cars…"

"Don't forget the boat."

She rolled her eyes, but she smiled again. "Who could forget the boat? I know we're going to be working. But I'm determined to have fun. I haven't had time away since…" She swallowed. "Since before," she finished decisively.

Although it probably wasn't a smart thing to do, Eric reached over and laced his fingers with hers. For a long moment, her hand was stiff in his and then, just when he'd decided this was another bad idea, her grip tightened around his. That spark flowed between them, but it was okay. Not a seduction. Here, in the car, they could hold hands and it would be all right.

"Sofia," he said softly, setting the bag of food on the floor and scooting over to her. "I'm so sorry."

Again, it was another long moment before she relaxed into him, her head against his shoulder. He closed his eyes and savored the feeling of her weight on his body. "It's…it's getting better. The job helps."

"Good." That was the most important thing, right? That he was giving her a way forward. That was the way he could help her best.

Her chest rose and fell as she took a deep breath and then, looking up at him, she said, "You help, Eric."

Up close, her eyes were a rich brown, shimmering and sweet, like the finest of brandies. He could get drunk on her, he realized.

He didn't know if she was leaning up to him or he was reaching down to her. Or both. He was only dimly aware of cupping her cheek with his hand and stroking his thumb over it. "I just want to make everything better for you," he murmured, staring in fascination as her eyes darkened. "That's what friends are for."

"Yes," she said, her voice little more than a whisper against his lips. "Friends."

Then she was kissing him and he was kissing her and it was intoxicating. She tasted sweet and spicy and hot. His temperature began to climb and it had nothing to do with artificial flavorings.

This wasn't like their first kiss. Not even close. Because this wasn't a tentative touching of lips with their eyes squeezed shut, both holding their breath.

This kiss was everything. He traced the seam of her lips with his tongue and Sofia sighed into his mouth, opening for him. He dipped his tongue into her mouth, searching for her taste underneath.

Sofia kissed him with a wild sort of abandon, like a woman starving for air who'd just surfaced above the waves. *Ah*, he thought, *there she was.* She tasted complex and sweet, just like the woman herself.

He shifted so he could wrap his arm around her shoulders and pull her in closer before he went back to kissing her. His blood hummed in his veins as the weight of her breasts pressed against his side. Shifting, he cupped one in his hand, the weight of her heavy and warm in his palm. Sofia moaned against his mouth as he stroked her. When her nipple went tight under his touch, he had to bite back his own groan. She was so responsive. God, she'd be amazing when she let go.

He wanted her to let go *now*. Still teasing her nipple, he sank his free hand into her hair, tilting her head so he could let his mouth drift down her neck until he found her pulse. It wasn't weak or irregular. Instead, her heart was beating hard and fast as a soft moan broke free of her lips. *"Eric."*

This was right, he realized. Sofia was right where she belonged, in his arms. He was hard for her and wanted nothing more than to sink into her softness and make her cry out with satisfaction.

The car lurched sharply around a corner, throwing them both off balance. He clutched her by the shoulders until they were both steady.

Or steadier, anyway. Her eyes were glazed with

desire and he knew he wasn't in any better shape. All he could do was look down at her and think how much he wanted to do that again.

He didn't take the chance because just as he leaned forward, Sofia sat back. Her gaze cleared and that delicious desire was replaced with tight lines of worry. "Oh. Oh. That was…"

She touched her lips with the tips of her fingers and Eric had to resist the urge to replace her fingers with his lips. But he didn't get the chance because she retreated across from him. He had to drop his arm from around her shoulder, but he wasn't going to relinquish his hold on her that easily. He wrapped his fingers around hers again.

"A mistake," she finished weakly.

He managed not to scowl. "It didn't feel like a mistake to me." Why had he thought this would be easy? Because it wasn't going to be. "Is this the part where you tell me we can't do this?"

"We can't." But she didn't pull her hand away from his. "Eric, we really can't."

"Why not? I like you. More than like, actually," he admitted. "I haven't been able to stop thinking about you since you walked back into my office. Into my life."

"I can't fall again," she said, her voice breaking. She turned to look at him, her eyes bright with tears. "I have to…" She swallowed and looked away again. "I have a job to do. I don't want to risk that."

He rolled his eyes. "Your job has nothing to do with any of this."

That got him a sharp look. Funny how it made him want to smile. "Don't be intentionally dense, Eric. I need the job. I need to take care of my family. I need to keep moving forward. You're paying me too much money—"

"Not that again," he huffed.

"And I can't risk that. Not for something as selfish as…" She swallowed again. "As short-term as sex."

Eric gaped at her in confusion. "Sofia. Look at me."

She didn't. She could be stubborn, his Sofia. "This is exactly like the salary argument, Eric. You can afford to do whatever you want. But I can't. I don't have hundreds of thousands—millions—of dollars to fall back on when this doesn't work."

He thought about that for a moment. Really, her argument was sound. She worked for him and he had a hard-and-fast rule about relationships with his staff—he didn't have them, period.

But Sofia wasn't just his office manager. She was his friend. Their relationship had started long before she'd begun to work for him—and he was beginning to realize he wanted it to last long afterward. "When was the last time you had sex?"

"Really?" she snapped, jerking her hand from his. "You're going to ask me *that*?"

"After that kiss? You're damn right I'm going to ask that. When was the last time you put your needs first?" Because he was willing to bet money that Sofia was low on her own to-do list.

She squeezed her eyes shut, her lips trembling. "Don't."

He could read the truth on her face. She hadn't been with anyone since her husband had died. A year and a half was a long time to go without a little loving.

He wanted to crush her in his arms and tell her everything would be okay—but hell. She'd been widowed and he'd been left at the altar and he couldn't promise her that everything would work out just so.

That didn't mean he wasn't going to try, though. He wasn't promising her forever, after all. Just the weekend. "I'm trying to understand, babe. You need to take care of your family. I get that. But who takes care of you?" He knew her mother worried about her, too. But being mothered wasn't the same thing as putting herself first.

She swallowed hard. "You're not going to fight fair, are you?"

"Of course not." She almost smiled at that—but not quite. "This weekend—let me take care of you. Which," he added, stroking his thumb along the side of her hand, "I'm already doing. I can't wait to see what dresses you decided on."

"Not the same," she muttered, yet he couldn't help but notice that she was still holding his hand, still submitting to his touch.

"Let's have fun this weekend," he went on. "Just

two old friends spending time together. No strings." He leaned over and nuzzled her hair with his nose. God, she smelled so good. He wanted to devour her. "Let me put you first, Sofia. You won't have to worry about anything."

She didn't answer for the longest time. "I don't know if I can do that. Not like you can."

That hurt more than he wanted it to. "Like me?"

"I can't be...casual." But she rested her head on his shoulder and it only made sense for him to tuck his arm around her again. "I mean... I don't know what I mean."

Eric let that thought roll around in his head. He assumed she knew about his ex-fiancée. Had she heard about the aftermath of the broken wedding? He'd gone through several high-profile, short-lived romances afterward before he'd burned himself out on meaningless sex. He hadn't exactly loved Prudence, but he'd at least cared for her, and sex without that caring wasn't the same. A physical release, yeah. But it hadn't been enough. He'd needed more.

Sofia in his arms felt like *more*.

His body ached for hers but for more than just a release—for both of them. He wanted to make her smile and laugh and...

He just wanted to make things right again. For her and maybe for him. For them both.

He kissed her head and did the right thing. "It's okay. We don't have to fool around." His body strained in protest but he ignored it. He wanted Sofia almost past the point of reason—but friends didn't pressure friends into sex.

She snorted in what he hoped was amusement.

"But," he went on, "if you change your mind, you let me know. Because I care about you, Sofia. I won't hurt you."

She was silent, but she let him hold her all the same. "Friends, right?"

"Right," he agreed. Friends were great. Friends with benefits were even better. But he managed to keep his mouth shut. "Always friends."

She sighed and leaned into him even more. "Thank you," she whispered.

And although it wasn't sex, there was something to just holding her that made Eric close his eyes and savor the moment.

He stroked Sofia's hair. She sighed again and even that small noise made him feel good. Great, even.

He needed this. He needed her and even if this was as far as it got, it was enough. For now.

The car bumped into a pothole and Sofia's cheek crinkled against the drawings her children had made for him. It was entirely possible, he realized, that he needed those babies, too. Their laughter, their hugs. Their joy. He needed that innocence in his life again. He was tired of being a cynic, holding himself apart from people because they'd disappoint him every single time.

He and Sofia stayed like that and Eric let himself enjoy the feel of her body pressed against his. Even this almost platonic touch felt right. She belonged in his arms.

How could he convince her of that?

Nine

"Almost there," Eric said, his voice low and close to her ear.

All Sofia could do was nod miserably as she leaned heavily on his arm.

"I can walk," Meryl protested weakly from just ahead of them.

"I know you can," Steve replied, sounding almost normal, "but no one needs to watch you bounce off the walls." With that, he swept his wife's legs out from underneath her and cradled her to his chest.

It wasn't much of a comfort that Sofia wasn't the only one who'd suffered mightily on the flight to St. Louis. The landing had been a terrifying exercise in flying during a storm and there'd been no way to push back against a panic attack. It'd been so bad that she'd forgotten how to breathe and had actually blacked out for a second.

Steve had gotten sick and Meryl looked like she needed a doctor. Even Eric, who was no doubt used to flying all over the place in that tiny aircraft as well as riding the waves on his boat, looked a little green around the gills.

Sofia's legs felt like rubber bands and her heart was still skipping at a weird rhythm—and they'd been on the ground for almost forty-five minutes. She hadn't had the strength to protest when Eric had slung his arm around her waist and held her up. She leaned into him, barely managing to keep hold of the bottle of ginger ale. She wasn't sure it was helping. She had no idea where her luggage was and she honestly didn't care.

"I know it's going to push us off schedule," Eric said loudly so Steve and Meryl could hear him, "but I think we all need a break. Can we afford two hours?"

"No," Meryl said, although she sounded like she was trying not to cry.

"Yes," Eric said more firmly. "Look at it this way, Meryl—no one would expect us to have landed during that storm, anyway. We had a flight delay, that's all. We still have all day tomorrow, too."

Meryl moaned pitifully, which made Steve croon to her.

The sound made Sofia's heart skip another beat, but not due to motion sickness. It was good, old-fashioned jealousy. God, she missed having someone who'd pick her up—literally or figuratively, it didn't much matter—when life knocked her sideways.

Just then, Eric leaned down to her, his arm tightening around her waist and his voice for her ears only. "There's your room, Sofia."

And even though it wasn't the same and Eric wasn't hers, she leaned into him even more because she felt terrible and Eric was the strength she needed right now and whatever happened this weekend, they would always be friends. Even if she fell a little more in love with him, they were friends.

The Nortons' room was across the hall from hers. "Where's your room?" she asked as Eric fumbled with her key card.

"Next door." He got her door open and basically set her inside, one hand still around her waist. He pivoted back to where Steve had gotten his door open. "Take as long as you guys need," Eric said quietly, as if Meryl wasn't right there. "It's better to be late than be ill during the meetings."

"I'll be fine…" But Steve closed the door and cut off Meryl's weak protest.

Eric pivoted Sofia into her hotel room. "I'm so sorry I'm such a mess," she said, knowing it was pointless to apologize but apparently unable to help herself.

Eric snorted as he sat her on the bed. "I'm sorry the flight sucked. That was one of the roughest landings I've ever had. Wasn't entirely sure the plane was going to hold together."

Her breath caught in her throat. She'd wondered the same thing, right about the time she'd stopped breathing. "Maybe we can take the train home?" she said, trying to make a joke and failing.

"The weather is supposed to be clearer on Sunday," he promised. "If it looks bad, we can make alternative arrangements." Then he knelt before her and picked up one of her feet. Sofia was aware that her pretty new silk top was plastered to her back with sweat and the rain had done a number on her hair and she probably looked one step removed from a drowned rat. She certainly didn't feel much better than one.

But then Eric moved. Slowly, he slid the cuff of her trouser up and pulled her brand-new Stuart Weitzman flat off her foot. There wasn't anything strange about him seeing her bare leg. It was just a leg. God only knew he'd seen that and more back when they'd spent half a summer splashing in a pool.

But the fact that Eric was removing her shoes for her? Undressing her?

Heat flashed down her back again, which was just ridiculous. This was not a seduction. She looked like hell and felt worse and they were supposed to be getting ready for meetings with the mayor and the board of aldermen and she was not letting Eric distract her with all his tenderness and certainly not with these...

Eric's fingertips gently caressed her calf and stroked along the top of her foot. The touch sent sparks of heat arcing up her body, burning her with desire. Her eyes fluttered shut and she had to brace her arms against the bed to keep from toppling into him.

His hands moved over her ankles, up her calves again. He warmed her skin with his palms, a strong and steady touch, and she couldn't help but think back to that kiss in the car, the one that had managed to awaken every single sexual need and desire she'd locked away over the last year and a half.

With Eric kneading the muscles of her legs, slowly moving up higher and higher, she no longer felt clammy and sick. She felt...

Good. Warm and safe and cared for. God, she'd missed feeling this way.

"Sofia," he said, his voice soft.

She wasn't sure if it was a question or not. And honestly, it didn't matter. They were friends, weren't they? And friends helped each other out. They had fun together. They comforted each other when things went wrong—and that plane ride had been very, very wrong.

Friends didn't let something like a few billion dollars or a private jet or luxury clothing get in the way of a friendship.

And really, once the trappings of money were removed—weren't they just a man and a woman? Weren't they made to fit together?

God, how she wanted to be comforted. To be touched like Eric was touching her now. She wanted to be the one taking the attention and affection instead of giving them.

"Sofia?" he said again, his voice sending low flutters through her belly.

Really, no matter what the question was, the answer was simple. "Yes."

His hands slid to a stop on the curve of her calves. Funny how she'd never really thought of calves as being particularly sensual until now. "Will you lie down and rest for a bit?"

She looked at him then. One of the most powerful men in Chicago—and quite possibly the country, to say nothing of the world—was on his knees before her, waiting for her answer. She uncurled her fingers from where she'd fisted the bedclothes and reached out to stroke his cheek. It was still early—not even eleven yet—and his jaw was smooth. "Only if you join me."

His eyes widened as he sucked in air. "Give me a few." With that, he pushed back off his heels. She heard a door open and shut and then she was alone.

Sofia dropped her head in her hands. She could still feel his hands on her legs, stroking and caressing her. She could still feel his arm around her waist, refusing to let her stumble through the hotel. For that matter, she could still feel his hand surrounding hers, holding on through the turbulence. He'd refused to let go.

She could still feel his lips against hers, his tongue tracing the path of her lips, her name soft on his breath. Eric had kissed her like she was the air he couldn't breathe without.

He was taking care of her. He wanted her to rest.

He was going to come back in here.

And she still looked like hell.

That thought finally got her to move. She downed the rest of her ginger ale and took stock. This was a really nice hotel room—king-size bed with a plush duvet, a velvet-covered sofa next to a coffee table and a television almost as big as David had ever bought. She went to the bathroom—even the toiletries were top-of-the-line. Of course they were. Eric Jenner wouldn't settle for less.

She recoiled at her reflection. Her hair had come loose from the bun and her makeup was shot. And yet, Eric had still sat there, staring up at her as if she were the only woman in the world. The shirt was a total loss, so she stripped it off, leaving her in only her camisole. And she didn't want to nap—or do anything else—in these trousers. Quickly, she washed her face—but then she remembered she didn't have her toiletry kit. Her luggage was being delivered separately by a bellhop.

She'd never stayed in a hotel that had bellhops who carried up one danged suitcase before. It was probably a great thing—but she really needed her stuff now.

She was using the facilities when there was a knock on the door. "One second," she called out, washing her hands quickly. But then she heard voices, both male.

Wait, what?

She cracked open the bathroom door to see Eric standing in an open door that…led to his room? Oh. *Oh.* Her room was connected to his. Of course it was. He had an executive suite. And her room was right next to his.

It shouldn't be a big deal, that he could walk into her room or she into his. It wasn't anything more intimate than removing her shoes, for God's sake. But it felt like the last barrier to truly spending the weekend in his arms had just been removed. They didn't have to walk out into the hall where Steve and Meryl might hear or see them.

Eric said, "Yes, that one goes in here. The other one goes in my room," as he looked up. When he saw her, his face softened as his gaze took in her face, her now-bare arms. He held up a finger to her, the universal sign for *hold on.*

She nodded and shut the door again, collapsing back against it. Their rooms connected. He wanted her. He'd already started to undress her.

She wanted him. Oh, how she wanted him.

But even as that thought occurred to her, she caught her reflection in the mirror. Her color was almost back to normal and she didn't look like she was on the verge of passing out again. Her hair wasn't great, though, so she unpinned it and combed it out with her fingers. She couldn't sleep with it pulled back like that, anyway.

She heard a door shut and then Eric said, "Do you need anything from your bag?"

"No," she fibbed. "I'll be right out."

"No rush."

Oh, but it felt like a rush. If she were going to throw herself at Eric—and that did look more and more likely—she would be jeopardizing her job and putting both of them in an awkward position. Steve and Meryl were right across the hall, so the risk of gossip spreading in the office was huge.

But damn it all, she needed him. She needed a weekend where she wasn't going through the motions of looking fine. She wanted to *be* fine and she knew Eric could give her that. He already had.

Sofia took one last look at her reflection. The hair was okay. She would prefer a little under-eye concealer, but the whole look wasn't too bad.

Have fun. Smile for yourself. That's what her mom had said. And Eric? He'd said nearly the same thing, adding in that he wanted to take care of her. And it was so clear from his actions in the last few hours that he didn't just mean a satisfying romp in bed. He really was taking care of her.

Her resolve set, she opened the door and stepped out.

The room was empty.

Ten

Sofia hesitated in the doorway of the suite. Not only was Eric's room much bigger than hers was, it was much grander. There was a dining room table set for four with fine china and crystal goblets. The kitchen—not a kitchenette, but a real kitchen with full-size stainless steel appliances and granite countertops—was off to the left. She took another step in, her feet sinking into the plush carpeting. The couches in the sitting area were similar to the one in her room, but they were longer and deeper and had luxurious-looking throw pillows on them. This place was far more spacious than the apartment she'd lived in growing up.

Okay, she thought. If she had to arrange travel for Eric in the future, this was the sort of room he needed. She'd do well to keep that in mind. She was trying to be a professional here. True, a barefoot professional in a camisole, but a professional none-theless.

Then all thoughts of professionalism came to a screeching halt when Eric appeared in a doorway across the room. He'd unbuttoned his shirt and was working his cuff links loose. Even though he had on a white T-shirt underneath, there was something about seeing him unbuttoned that sent another shiver down Sofia's back.

Her nipples tightened underneath her camisole at the sight of him and that physical reaction had *noth-ing* to do with friendship.

She crossed her arms in front of her traitorous nipples. "So this is the kind of room you need when you travel?"

He notched an eyebrow at her, which made him look amused. "It is. In fact, when I come to St. Louis, I usually stay in this suite. I like the views of the park." He motioned to the windows over his shoul-der. Sofia had a view of buildings, but Eric had a sweeping vista of a huge green park.

"The next best thing to a view of a lake?"

His smile deepened and she got the feeling that she'd pleased him. "It is."

They looked at each other for a moment. She wasn't sure what she was supposed to do in a situa-tion like this. After all, they weren't acting in their capacity as boss and employee, but they weren't quite operating within the normal bounds prescribed by "old friends," either. She felt stuck. "I didn't realize our rooms connected," she said dumbly.

"I hope it's okay with you that I opened them up?" Then he began to slide his shirt off his shoulders. No, that was not the same body she remembered from all those years ago. Eric had filled out. His white T-shirt strained across his chest and his biceps. He wasn't overly muscled, but he wasn't lean and lanky anymore, either. She smiled as she looked at his biceps. There was an inch of paler skin showing just below the cuff of the sleeve before his arm turned a deep golden brown. She stared in fascination at that strip of skin. Redheads with a tan were so very rare.

He was so rare.

She had no right to be in this deluxe suite with him, no right to be staring at that strip of skin. She had no right to him—but she wanted him all the same. Just for the weekend. Just for herself.

Sofia took a deep breath and let her arms fall to her side. "Why wouldn't it be?"

His eyes darkened as his gaze fell to her breasts. Her nipples tightened even more, jutting out through the thin fabric of the camisole. She swore she heard him growl. But instead of pouncing, he said, "Feeling better?"

"A little."

He moved closer to her and she stepped into him. They stopped just short of each other and he lifted his hand to brush her hair away from her face. "Hi," he said softly, cupping her cheek in his palm.

She leaned into his touch. They'd spent the whole morning together, but this? She didn't feel like she was standing in front of Eric Jenner, eligible bachelor billionaire. Without his bespoke shirts and other trappings of wealth, she was just standing with Eric, her friend. She hesitated before she jumped into the gap, resting her hands on the narrow vee of his waist. His body radiated heat underneath her hands, all the hotter now because he wasn't wearing his jacket and shirt. "Were we going to lie down?"

"Absolutely." He stroked his thumb over the apple of her cheek, his gaze on her lips. "Were we going to sleep?"

Heat flashed through her body, stronger and more insistent than what she'd felt in the car. Then, she'd been nervous about leaving the twins and the flight. All of that was behind her now—but the flight had left her drained. "We had a rough landing, Eric. And I don't get to nap very much. Let me just…" She stepped in closer, her breasts pressing against his chest. Her nipples ached as they brushed against him. She leaned her head on his shoulder. Dear God, she'd missed the feeling of a man. "Will you hold me?"

His arms did not come around her and for a paralyzing second, she thought he would say no. But before she could back away, Eric bent down and swept her legs out from under her, just like Steve had done to Meryl. "Eric!"

"I've got you," he said close to her ear. It was what she needed to hear. More than that, it was what she needed to believe.

And, as Eric cradled her lovingly, she did believe it. She relaxed into his arms and let him carry her weight. "Pick a room," he told her. "Mine or yours?"

She didn't have to think about it. "Yours." That way, if whatever this was didn't pan out, she could go back to her own room and not have to smell him on her pillows.

She should not be doing this but she seemed powerless to do anything but let him carry her to the very big bed. "Do you mind if I take my trousers off? I don't want to wrinkle them."

Such an innocent-sounding request, but there was no mistaking the fact that he'd be one step closer to naked. That didn't stop her from saying, "Go right ahead."

He sat her on the edge of the bed and stepped back. She looked up at him—and *not* at the buttons he was undoing. He paused and touched her cheek again.

She couldn't hold back the happy sigh. It'd been so long. She knew she was being dramatic but it almost felt like her first time again—and in a way, it was. Her first time with Eric.

Everything about her wanted to reach out for him, pull him in close and trust that he would be right there if she needed him, however she needed him.

Instead, she stood and undid her own button and

zipper. The white trousers were more or less a total loss—the rain had seen to that. But she needed to be close to Eric right now, needed the comfort his body could provide. What she was feeling for him wasn't just about sex. Not entirely, anyway. It was about something more.

She tried not to stare at his bulge as he shucked his pants, but it wasn't easy because... Oh, my.

Grinning to herself, she kicked her trousers aside and gave thanks to Clarice, who had seen fit to include undergarments in her total wardrobe makeover. Instead of the serviceable cotton she normally wore Sofia had on a pair of high-cut silk panties with lace around the waist. They were a sheer nude color, all the better to be worn under a pair of white pants— and the first thong that she had ever owned. Clarice would hear of nothing else because she claimed that a visible panty line would just *ruin* the look.

Sofia felt exposed and vulnerable. But it wasn't a bad feeling, she realized. Instead of anxiety, tendrils of anticipation uncurled through her limbs, making her body feel heavy and needy.

For him. For the gorgeous man waiting for her in a very large bed. He pulled the covers back and slid in first, patting the bed beside him. "Come here."

Sofia had not had a wild adolescence. She'd been raised in a fairly strict religious household that frowned upon casual dating and sex and besides, an accidental pregnancy would have made achieving her goals harder. She had been a virgin when she'd started dating David. She'd never been in bed with anyone else.

Except for now. Was there any turning back once she slid next to Eric and put her arms around his waist? Was there any hope of holding a part of herself back so she wouldn't fall in love with him all over again? Because if she were lucky, this…connection would last the weekend—and not a moment longer. A weekend was long enough to have some fun and reclaim her sexuality with Eric's help without it blowing up in her face. For a few days, she could pretend she belonged not only in his life, but in his bed.

A weekend would be enough. It had to be.

Eric's gaze drifted over her camisole, her bare legs. His eyes darkened and he held out his hand for her and she knew there was no turning back. She scooted over to him. He pulled the covers up over them and settled her in the curve of his arm. She wrapped her own arm around his waist and slung her leg over his. And then, for the first time in what felt like months, she exhaled. "Eric…"

"Shhh," he murmured, stroking her hair. "Just rest for a bit. I'll be here when you wake up." And although it didn't seem like she would be able to— not with their bare legs intertwined, not with his arms around her—Sofia closed her eyes and drifted off, feeling safe and, somehow, that everything was going to be all right.

Eric felt the moment Sofia slipped off to sleep. Her muscles relaxed and she sank into him, warm and soft. It was strange, how easy it was to hold her like this. His body hummed at a high pitch, attuned to everything about her. The softer she got, the harder he got.

Was he preparing for one of the biggest business meetings of his career? Was he looking toward the future at all? No. Instead, all he could think about—feel—was the curve of Sofia's breasts pressing against his side, her smooth leg thrown over his. She was wearing a see-through thong, which meant there was next to nothing between them. He could feel the heat of her body against his hip, smell the warmth of her skin.

This was torture, plain and simple. And he'd suffer it willingly because even with his dick throbbing, holding her was one of the most satisfying things he'd ever done.

How long had he told the Nortons? Two hours? It wasn't going to be enough. It'd never be enough time, not when he was tucked into bed with Sofia, his body straining for hers. And the hell of it was, he might just keep right on straining. Just because they were half-naked and wrapped around each other didn't mean that Sofia wanted anything else from him. She'd asked him to hold her and by God, that was what he was going to do.

Luckily, his watch was on the hand he could look at without disturbing her. Right before the bellhop had shown up with their luggage, he'd sent a quick message to the mayor's executive assistant, stating the weather had delayed them and he would be in touch when they were able to make it. But he figured that meant he and Sofia only had an hour at most. Then they needed to get up and get changed and go back to being Mr. Jenner and Ms. Bingham, boss and office manager. And they had to stay that way until…

He mentally ran through the schedule. They had meetings with the mayor and the city planner this afternoon. This evening was a formal dinner with several members of the state government, including the lieutenant governor. Tomorrow was more meetings and site visits with negotiations. He needed Meryl to be his bulldog, Steve to convince everyone what they wanted was doable, and Sofia to be his eyes and ears. After all, this was a *huge* deal. St. Louis was ripe for the picking and if Eric played his cards right, he would be richer than his wildest dreams.

It was damned hard to care about that right now. He was already rich beyond his wildest dreams and following that carefully planned schedule meant he'd have to leave this room. He'd have to put distance between himself and Sofia and spend the afternoon and the next several days without holding her hand. Without touching her at all. He didn't know how he was supposed to do that.

If Meryl and Steve weren't here, Eric would claim the flu and cancel the whole weekend. But people depended on him. All of his employees, not to mention all of the locals he would hire for construction.

He'd be sinking a lot of money into this project and it would do a lot of good. He couldn't blow that off for something as selfish as a weekend in Sofia's arms.

Besides, he was violating his own code of not getting involved with his employees. True, it was hard to remember that when he was with Sofia. But she did work for him. Technically, right now, they were on the clock. And mostly naked in bed together.

His last thought before he drifted off was that maybe he shouldn't have hired her.

Eric floated in the space between awake and asleep. He couldn't wait to get Eddy and Addy out on his boat. They might need to bring along a nanny to watch the kids. He wanted the kids to have fun, but he wanted Sofia to have a good time, too—and it might be hard to do that if she were constantly chasing after the twins. Because if the kids liked it and Sofia had a good time, then she'd come out boating with him again. And he wanted that.

How good would Sofia look on his boat, stretched out on a lounge chair, her body clad in a bikini, the sun kissing her skin like he wanted to? Instead of kissing her, he pulled her down into the cabin and stretched her out on the bed. She sighed as he put his hands on her body and the noise went straight through him. Her legs were long and shapely and he stroked his palm from her knees to her thigh and her hip and back down again. And again, and again. He couldn't get enough of her. Maybe he never would.

As he massaged her skin, she turned into him, her body almost on top of him. Now he could reach her backside. She had a woman's curves and all he could think was *lush*. Hopefully, when they woke up, he'd have a chance to do this in real life. He wanted his hands all over—not just stroking, but grabbing and feeling and knowing her, all of her.

His dream Sofia stretched against him and Eric half lifted, half rolled her onto his chest. Now he could grab her backside with both hands, filling his palms with her flesh. His fingertips grazed the lace edge of the barely there panties and he shifted her body so the hard length of his arousal was pressed against her very center.

His dream Sofia gasped, a noise that cut right through Eric's daze. He blinked and then blinked again. The bedroom cabin of his ship resolved into a familiar hotel room—but Sofia was still on top of him.

Holy crap, this wasn't a dream. Sofia was straddling him, staring down at him through heavy-lidded eyes. She pushed her hands through her hair and arched her back, driving her weight down onto his erection. Stunned, Eric was helpless to do anything but grind against her. She gasped again.

God, she felt so good, so damned right on top of him. He was afraid to say something, afraid to break the spell that would wake them both up from this dream. So he kept his mouth shut as he gripped her bottom in his hands and dragged her up along his erection again.

She moaned softly, so quietly he almost didn't hear it. She kept that little noise of satisfaction deep in her throat and he wanted to let it out. He wanted to swallow it and take it inside of himself and let it rattle around until it drove him past all reason.

She shifted and he shifted with her, pressing against her center again and again. Her back arched, thrusting her breasts out. He grabbed the hem of her camisole and yanked it over her head.

And his head fell back against the pillows as he stared at her body. *Lush* was still the only word he could think of. Soft and curved and wearing a sheer lace bra. He could see the wide dark circles of her nipples.

There was too much and not enough and it completely short-circuited his brain. He couldn't move, he couldn't think. All he could do was stare at her. Worship her.

He worshipped just a moment too long. Sofia dropped her gaze as she put one arm across her breasts, the other across her rounded stomach. "I know, I know. Having the twins changed me and I'm not—"

Eric didn't know what she was going to say, not exactly—but he knew he disagreed with it completely because she was perfect. He sat up and cut her off with a hard kiss. Sofia made a little squeaking noise, but then her arms came around his neck and she held on to him for balance as he slid his hands up and down her back. Then he began to work the catch of her bra, kissing her the entire time. She sank her fingers into his hair and refused to let go. He liked that she was a little aggressive and *very* sure of herself. The kiss in the car this morning had been a promise of things to come but this? This was a promise delivered.

The catch on her bra gave and he peeled the lace away. He didn't want to break the kiss, but he couldn't resist lowering his head to those beautiful breasts. They were full and heavy and he loved everything about them. Even the little white stretch marks along the sides—they were perfect because they were a part of Sofia. "Are these off-limits?" he asked as he kissed along the swells.

"No," she said, throwing her head back and giving him better access. "I only nursed for a year."

"You are the most beautiful woman I've ever seen," he murmured as he kissed the edge of her nipple and then swept his tongue over the tip. It went tight against his mouth and he couldn't help the rumble of satisfaction that built low in his chest. He was already drunk on her. He had no intention of jumping on the wagon now.

"Oh my God, Eric," she moaned, clutching his head to her breasts.

Her hips kept shifting back and forth, grinding down on his erection. With one hand steady on her backside, he slid his thumb down between her legs, over the silk of her panties until he found the center of her pleasure. She jolted as if he'd shocked her and he smiled against her skin before adding his teeth to her nipples.

"Oh, Eric," she gasped, letting her weight settle over his thumb.

He began to rub in small circles as he nipped and sucked at her breasts. They found a rhythm together as he worked her body. All he wanted to do was flip her over and drive into her heat over and over again until they were both spent and sated and then, once he'd caught his breath, he wanted to do it again.

But he wanted to give this to her first. No demands, just the gift of pleasure. Just her trusting him. Just him earning her trust.

Like he was doing right now. She was letting him love her and he was making the most of it. Dimly, in the back of his mind, he knew there were good reasons to not do this. But he couldn't come up with any of those reasons right now and besides, it was a little too late to keep his hands off her. That ship had definitely sailed.

As she shifted her hips back and forth, her warm heat stroked over his erection even as he stroked her body. The pressure was intense and amazing and when she pulled on his hair, forcing his face up so she could kiss him, he felt her entire body go tight and hard around his. "Let go, Sofia," he murmured against her lips.

And she did. Her thighs clamped around his waist

and heat flooded her center as she came for him. The force of her climax was so strong that, amazingly, it triggered his own release. He hadn't been this excited, this eager, since he'd been a teenager discovering girls for the first time.

But that's what this felt like. He had just discovered something new and amazing.

He'd found Sofia.

Eleven

Sofia collapsed onto Eric's chest, breathing hard. His hand was still pressed between her legs and her stomach was damp where it rested against the waistband of his briefs. The orgasm ricocheted around her body like a bullet fired into a metal tank. She was hot and tight and loose all at the same time and it was *wonderful*. Simply amazing.

And that was when she realized that she might be completely in love with him. Damn his hide.

Her breathing was ragged and she couldn't seem to stop shaking. But in a good way. The best way. But it was different, too. She'd loved sex with her husband but that felt like a different life. She hadn't anticipated how different her body would feel straddling Eric as he brought her to completion. His mouth on hers, his teeth on her breasts?

She shuddered again. It hadn't been the same. Even that thought felt almost like a betrayal, though. She'd loved David with her whole heart and soul—and body.

But she might be in love with Eric.

God, her head was a mess. And the more those delicious little shivers of satisfaction faded away, the more her brain started to freak out. Good Lord—had she and Eric really just done *that*?

It'd all happened like a dream unfolding. She'd been asleep and then not quite asleep, Eric's warm body next to hers. Her body had filled with a languid warmth and the space between her legs had grown heavy and she had *wanted*. It'd been so long since she'd wanted. Desire and sensuality—they hadn't been a part of her life since David had died.

If it were anyone else, it wouldn't have happened. It wouldn't have gotten even close to happening because she never would've stripped down to her panties and climbed into bed with anyone else. But this wasn't some random stranger spouting stale pickup lines and vague promises he had no intention of keeping. This was Eric.

He'd held her children and made them laugh. He'd kissed her in the car. He'd promised that whatever happened in this bed was separate from them working together. He'd literally seen her at her worst—on multiple occasions—and yet he was still here, giving her a mind-blowing orgasm.

She didn't just want to get laid in the service of vague sexual frustration. She wanted *him*. And she could have him. So she had.

Sort of.

His arms came around her and he held her tightly. "God, Sofia," he said, his chest still heaving from the climax. He sounded happy and…relieved? "I mean…" His voice trailed off and he kissed her head.

No, she didn't know what he meant. Other than he'd enjoyed it, too—which made her feel good. Although she hadn't done much.

Just straddled him. Just ground her hips down along his length—his very impressive length. Just cried out his name. Her body quivered, a reaction she couldn't control.

He shifted, somehow pulling her closer and that, at least, calmed her racing thoughts. She closed her eyes and ducked her chin against his shoulder and tried her hardest just to be in this moment. She hadn't had sex in so long, but she could still feel that passion, that need. And she could still be satisfied. That was the important thing here.

Not the fact that she had no idea what she was supposed to do next. Compliment him on his skills? Make some saucy comment about how she couldn't wait to do that and more this evening? Tell him how she felt about him? She and David had always said they loved each other afterward. Every single time.

Her mouth opened as if on automatic, but she snapped it back shut. Even if Eric had made her fall in love with him, she couldn't very well tell him that. Because he'd promised to take care of her, to have some fun with her. To keep this weekend separate from everything else. Love didn't figure into any of those things. In fact, it would probably ruin everything.

She didn't want to remind him that, outside of this room, they didn't belong together.

When she couldn't come up with anything reasonable to say, she felt Eric's arms tighten around her. "Babe? Are you okay?"

She let out a little laugh. No, she wasn't okay. Not even close. She couldn't even commit to a friends-with-benefits weekend without overthinking the whole danged thing. "Yeah. Just…"

"Been a while?"

She nodded, grateful to hide behind that half-truth. She *was* a little rusty, after all. "Now what?"

"I don't know about you, but I need a shower." Just then, his watch beeped. "Hang on." She tried to roll off him, but he put a hand on her lower back to keep her where she was before answering his watch. "Yes?"

"Eric? I've managed to get Meryl up and into the shower. She's arguing with me, so I think she's fine."

Sofia stayed very still as Steve spoke. Her face was burning. It wasn't as if Steve had walked in on them, but it felt like it.

Why couldn't she have decided to do this whole benefits thing when she wasn't on a business trip?

But then again, when else was she going to spend time with Eric?

Oh, what a mess.

"Are you guys sure you can make it through the afternoon?" Eric asked, sounding calm and professional and nothing like the man who had just brought her to orgasm with nothing more than his fingers.

"I think so. Give us another forty-five minutes and we should be ready."

"Sounds good," Eric agreed, but even as he said it, he lazily traced his fingertips up her bare back.

Then Steve asked, "Do you want me to tell Sofia?"

Eric still sounded perfectly normal when he said, "I'll let her know. We'll see you in a few." He ended the call and let his head fall back against the mattress. "I guess that means we have to get up."

"I guess it does," she said. Eric's calm was contagious, almost. Her heart was slowing down to a steady, reliable beat and she was breathing normally.

But she still had no idea how she was supposed to face the afternoon schedule. Before, it had seemed daunting, but now it felt almost impossible. How was she supposed to handle herself now?

Eric tilted her face up so she had to look at him. "Are you sure you're all right?"

She tried a confident smile. Given the way he notched an eyebrow at her, she was pretty sure she failed. "I don't know what to do next. I mean, about us. About this." She let out a strangled laugh. "And also about having dinner with the lieutenant governor tonight. None of this is normal for me, Eric. I don't fit in this world."

He stroked his thumb over her cheek and gave her a smile that, if she'd been standing, would've made her knees wobble. "You're going back to your room to take a shower and get changed. I'm going to do the same here. We're going to some meetings where Meryl will negotiate until she's blue in the face, Steve will make friends with everyone and I'll make grand promises that sound too good to be true, except I'll have all the numbers to back them up. All you have to do for the rest of the evening is smile and listen. You're the best listener I've ever met. Take notes on what's being whispered, when people look nervous or whatever. I want to know what's not being said, okay?"

"Okay."

He stroked his thumb over her cheek again. "If you feel awkward, compliment someone on their tie or their presentation or whatever. Can't go wrong with compliments. You do that and we'll be fine."

He sounded so damned confident about it, as if he actually believed she could pull this off. Preparing for today's meetings and tonight's dinner—that was where all her focus should be. It didn't matter how easily he thought she could do this—she knew darned good and well that today would be hard and tonight would be harder. She had no experience in high-level meetings, even less experience at high-stakes cocktail parties. Eric could be confident because that sort of thing came naturally to him. He breathed it, lived it every single day.

God, she hoped she didn't embarrass herself. But more than that, she hoped she didn't embarrass him. There was a real risk that if she did something wrong, she might cost him this deal.

And if that happened, after what they'd shared?

She'd never be able to look him in the eye again.

But now, there was no escaping the fact that they were still lying in bed together, almost naked, the sweat on her back starting to cool. She wanted him to warm her up all over again. "And after that?"

He held her gaze for a moment before he said in a quiet voice, "That's up to you. But this is a big bed," he went on, giving her a playful grin. "Plenty of room." To emphasize this, he patted around. "I might get lonely. Just saying."

She should say no. She should walk away while she still could, before they crossed that final line. If she were strong enough, she'd sleep alone tonight.

But just then, Eric cupped her face and brushed a tender kiss over her lips and she knew she wasn't going to be strong enough. She knew she'd be right back in his arms tonight.

"That would be tragic, wouldn't it?"

He leaned up to press a hard, quick kiss against her lips before he patted her bottom. "Devastating. But we've got a lot to do before then."

With a sigh, she rolled off him and out of bed. "Then we better get to it."

"Well," Eric said as the elevator doors closed behind them. "I think that went well."

It took almost everything Sofia had not to slump against the wall of the elevator. And frankly, she didn't have much left. Who would've thought that paying attention to conversations all day long with a smile plastered to her face would be so exhausting?

But that wasn't the only thing that had left her drained. The effort it took not to watch Eric, not to smile at him—not to show that she was aware of every single thing he did—had taken a lot out of her.

She hadn't wanted to look like a woman lusting after her boss. She had no idea if she'd made it.

Because she was *definitely* lusting after Eric.

She barely recognized the woman reflected in the mirrored walls of the elevator. The black-and-white lace patterned dress was working overtime, as was the strapless bra. She almost didn't look like the mother of twins, which was impressive.

If she threw a suit jacket over this dress, she could wear it to work. But for dinner tonight, she had tucked the pashmina shawl around her shoulders and left her arms bare.

Eric had noticed, too. She'd felt his gaze upon her all night long. Just like it was right now. He shifted closer to her so their shoulders were touching. In the reflection, he smiled at her and Sofia couldn't help but think, *We fit.*

Which was ridiculous. Just because his black suit and bright blue tie looked good with this dress absolutely did not mean that she fit with him. But it was enough to pretend for this weekend.

"Can we wait until morning to go over our notes?" Meryl asked, sounding drained.

Sofia startled. Were they supposed to be business professional after eight solid hours of meetings? Before she and Eric could pick up where they'd left off this afternoon?

Even throughout dinner—one of the finer meals she'd ever eaten—she'd been focused on listening. She was used to sleep deprivation. Anyone with small children was. But coloring with the kids required a much lower level of mental engagement than following along with a dinner conversation that encompassed state, federal and city ordinances.

But she hadn't made a fool of herself. She'd offered up a few compliments and paid attention and managed not to stare at Eric and think of nothing but his body against hers. Nothing tonight had come naturally to her, but she'd made it. It seemed that, for one weekend at least, she could pretend she belonged by Eric's side.

"Absolutely," Eric readily agreed. His fingertips brushed and then tangled with Sofia's. That simple contact went through her like a lightning bolt. Instantly, she was wide awake. "It's been a long day, but I'm so impressed at the way everyone recovered and I know that tomorrow, we'll be right back at it."

"Go, team," Steve said weakly, which made Meryl laugh.

Sofia managed a chuckle. Tomorrow would be another long day and she wasn't entirely sure she would be able to fake her way through it.

But tonight?

Tonight she would wrap her arms around Eric and be a little bit selfish. She could take what she needed instead of having to worry about what other people needed. It would be worth it, even if it were awkward tomorrow morning. She wanted to remember that she was Sofia, a woman with desires and needs.

She gave Eric's fingers a squeeze and felt a ripple of tension move up his arm. Then he let go of her hand as the elevator stopped at their floor. "What time is the first meeting tomorrow?" he asked as they filed out of the elevator and down the hall toward their rooms.

"Nine a.m." Sofia replied. And since everything had been pushed back today, there was no hoping for an extra hour tomorrow morning.

"Let's meet in my suite at eight for breakfast." He still sounded confident and alert, as if he could have lingered at the bar for another few hours.

She didn't want to linger at the bar. She wanted to linger in his bed, by God.

Meryl and Steve mumbled their agreements as they reached their room. Eric paused and looked back over his shoulder, making eye contact with Sofia. She bobbed her head, agreeing to the question he hadn't asked—at least not in words.

It didn't matter. The answer was still yes.

"Good night," she said to the hallway at large as she went into her room. She took a moment to use the bathroom and freshen up and then, still in her fancy dress, she opened the door on her side of the wall.

His side was already open. Quietly, she stepped into the room. Even that simple act had her pulse beating at a higher rhythm, which was still a new and exciting feeling to her. During that first year after David had passed, when she'd been struggling to care for her newborn twins, her sexuality had been in hibernation. She hadn't had the energy to miss it then, but when she'd begun to emerge from the fog of depression and sleep deprivation, she'd wondered if she would be capable of sexual desire again. It was almost like she'd forgotten how.

Then, this afternoon, Eric had made her shatter with nothing more than a well-placed touch and some passionate kisses. Which had been wonderful relief. She could still *feel*. That part of her hadn't died with David.

But she wanted more. She wanted it all.

She wanted Eric. And thank God, he was here for her.

This was just the weekend. On Monday, they'd go back to normal. She'd go to work and he'd go boating.

No more clothes, no more kisses in the back of his car. No more pictures of Eric cuddling her children.

No one would know. Especially not her mother.

Eric came out of his bedroom and, without breaking stride, crossed the room and pulled her into his arms. His mouth came down over hers, a kiss so hot that suddenly she had on far too much clothing. Luckily for her, he was hell-bent on rectifying that situation.

"All night long," he murmured against the delicate skin of her neck, making her pulse flutter wildly, "I've been staring at you in this dress."

"I like this dress." The zipper moved down her back one notch at a time as his mouth drifted down her neck to her cleavage at the exact same pace. Luxurious warmth built low in her body and radiated out. For the first time in so long, she was warm. God, she hoped Eric heated her up.

She went on, "It makes me look…"

Well, it made her look like she fit in his world.

"Correction," he said as he tugged the zipper down the rest of the way. Cool air kissed her back and she shivered, her nipples going hard. "You make the dress look amazing, Sofia." He took a step back, and the dress gaped at her chest. He ran his fingers under the straps then pulled them off her shoulders. "But you know what's better than you in this dress?"

"What?"

"You out of this dress."

The dress puddled at her waist and he stepped into her again, working it over her hips.

"Oh, Sofia," he breathed as the dress fell to the floor and she was left in nothing but a strapless bra, underwear and her shoes. His eyes warmed as he stepped back to look her over. "I thought I was ready, but I'm not."

Twelve

"**Y**ou're not?" Anxiety began to twist in her stomach again. *Please,* please *don't let this be a mistake in the making.*

But Eric cupped her cheeks in his palms, lifting her face to his. "I may never be ready for you, babe. You're always going to take my breath away, aren't you?"

And before she could reply to that sincere compliment—damn him and his sincere compliments—he lowered his mouth to hers again.

She lost herself in the give-and-take of their kiss. Somehow, they were moving, although she wasn't aware of taking any steps. Eric kicked out of his shoes and then she was pushing his shirt off his shoulders. He lost his pants in the doorway to the bedroom and she pulled his undershirt off next to the bed. Now it was her turn to step back and admire him. It made her smile to see that he had on black boxer briefs. Black was de rigueur for the evening, apparently.

Hopping on one foot and then the other, he peeled off his socks. There was something familiar and comforting about it and yes, silly. She'd watched him peel off his socks and shoes countless times when they used to throw themselves into the pool as kids.

It was ridiculous that something as simple as taking off his socks could make her relax, but it did. This was okay. Better than okay. He was still Eric and somewhere, deep inside, she was still Sofia. No matter how much it changed, that would always be the same.

She started to take her strappy heeled sandals off, but Eric said, "No, wait." Before she could figure out what he meant, he fell to his knees and set his hands against the buckle of the sandal.

This was the second time today he had been on his knees before her, undressing her slowly. And she knew in all truthfulness that she might not ever be ready for him, either. It didn't make sense, why he was putting so much effort into this. He could've had his pick of any woman in the world. Why was he here with her?

He got her sandals off and then sat back on his heels, staring up at her. "You doing okay?" Before she could answer, he leaned forward and pressed a kiss against her thigh.

She laced her fingers in his hair to balance herself. "I think so," she answered honestly before she realized he might take it the wrong way.

He paused. "We can stop."

She stared down at him. Even from this angle, she could see his erection straining against the waistband of his briefs. She'd felt it grinding against her earlier, his body hot and heavy for her.

"I don't want to stop," she told him, raking her fingers through his hair. "I want to feel good, Eric. I want to be selfish." And, although she didn't say it, she knew he understood—she didn't want to regret this.

More than that, she didn't want this to be somber and quiet. She was so tired of being serious, of feeling like the fate of the world rested on every single decision she made.

"And I want to have fun," she said, unable to stop her voice from wavering. "I need to have fun. With you. Please."

"I would do anything for you, Sofia," he said and dammit all, his voice was serious. "Anything, that is, except eat one of those fire-hot Takis again."

She surprised herself by laughing and he grinned. "Those things took a year off of my life," he went on, somehow sounding serious and yet completely ridiculous at the same time. "And the fact that you could eat them without crying? I wonder about you sometimes."

He pulled her underwear, working them down slowly over her hips. It might've made her self-conscious, but for every inch he crossed, he leaned up and pressed a kiss. And even as he did that slow and sensual seduction, he kept cracking jokes.

Had she seen when the lieutenant governor's tie accidentally dipped into his soup? Had she heard the dirty jokes Steve had been telling to the owners of a local construction company? Had she caught it when Eric tripped over the threshold of the restaurant and nearly took out the hostess?

Of course she had. She hadn't missed any of it. But she'd been afraid to laugh then, afraid to draw attention to herself.

But now? Her chest loosened as she was able to giggle at him, at the whole evening. People treated Eric like he was royalty, deigning to grace them with his presence, when he was just *Eric*. A man who occasionally threw boulders into a swimming pool and liked junk food and looked out for an old friend. He wasn't some high-and-mighty soulless billionaire.

Oh, God, she was completely in love with him, wasn't she?

No, this wasn't about love. This was about satisfaction and friendship and…and…sex. That's all. Nothing more. There couldn't be anything more.

"There," he said, coming to his feet and wrapping

his arms around her, working the clasp of her bra. "There's that smile I wanted to see."

Then the bra gave and she was completely nude before him for the first time. Unlike this afternoon, she successfully fought the urge to cover herself with her hands. Instead of focusing on herself, she turned her attention to him. "Your turn."

"You know what I regret?" he asked as she hooked her fingers into the waistband of his briefs and began to pull down.

"No?" She really didn't want to bring regrets into this.

He slid a finger under her chin so that even as she pushed his briefs down, she had no choice but to look in his eyes. "I regret that I missed the moment you transformed from a kid I used to know into the woman I want."

She pushed the waistband over his lean hips and the shorts fell away. "You didn't miss it," she told him, her hands finding his erection. She didn't need to see it to know that he was impressive and powerful. She could feel it for herself. He sucked in air as she encircled his girth with her hands.

"I didn't?"

Somehow, it did her good to hear him on the edge like this, his voice unsteady, his eyes dark with desire.

"It was the moment I walked into your building. It never would've happened before that exact moment in time." She worked her hands up and down his erection, feeling him come alive under her touch.

"I'm so glad I didn't miss it," he said and then his mouth was on her, his hands pulling her hair loose from the updo she'd managed all by herself.

"Me, too," she said and then they were falling into bed together, his body covering hers. She touched him everywhere. He was so hot and smooth and hard against her, flexing his hips and dragging his erection over her very center. He was driving her wild and God, it felt so good.

This wasn't a dream, not like this afternoon. But the rest of the world fell away, anyway. She didn't think of funerals or hospital bills or babies or jobs. As Eric skimmed his teeth over the base of her neck, all she could think about was how he wanted to devour her. When he teased her nipples to tight, hard points, all she could think about was that she wanted to share them with him. And when he stroked his fingers between her legs, finding the center of her pleasure and working it until her hips bucked against his and she cried out with need, all she could think was that she'd found herself. She'd found herself again with him.

"One moment," he said, peeling himself off her. She shivered as the cold air touched her heated skin.

"What's the matter?"

"Nothing." He went back to the doorway, where his pants were still crumpled on the floor. He pulled a condom out of his pocket and then prowled back toward her.

She got her first good look at Eric's body. Oh, he had grown up well. She had felt all of those muscles and skin against her, cupped him with her hands— but seeing was believing and she wasn't sure she believed that he was all hers.

"Did I ever tell you I like your tan lines?" she asked as he kneeled back on the bed and climbed between her legs.

"No, you didn't." He rolled the condom on and then came against her.

"You should wear sunscreen," she told him, running her hands up and down his biceps. "But you're a redhead with a tan, Eric. Someone rare and special. There's no one else like you in the world and I can't believe I have you all to myself right now."

She could feel him at the entrance of her body. She desperately wanted to flex her hips up and take him inside of her. But he was staring down at her with such tenderness that it was almost alarming.

"Sofia…" he said, and something in his tone made her breath catch in her throat.

Then he began to thrust into her and she knew that no matter how much he made her laugh or how good he made her feel, this was about so much *more* than just a little bit of fun.

He went slow, filling her inch by inch. Her body spasmed around his. Oh, it had been so long. And he felt so good that she wanted to cry with the relief.

He was breathing hard, his face buried against her neck and she thought he was shaking. For a long moment, they lay like that, joined but quiet in the intimacy of it all.

He said her name again softly. "Sofia."

"Yes," she whispered. It didn't really matter what the question was, after all. He was here with her and they were together and the answer was *yes*. Maybe it always would be.

He flexed his hips and she rose to meet him and together, they found a rhythm. Sofia wondered dimly if she should be doing more, trying harder. But there was something so freeing about laying back and letting him take care of everything. She didn't have to give and give and *give*, dammit, until there was nothing left for her. She could be selfish and greedy and take everything he had because right now, he was all hers.

"Tell me what you need, babe," Eric grunted, his breathing harsh. "Let me give it to you."

She needed so much—more than a night or even a weekend. She needed to make up for all the time she'd lost just getting by. She was tired of survival. She wanted to live.

She was finally going to. "Let's... Here. Lean back."

Eric did as she asked, sitting on his heels without pulling free of her body. "You feel so good," she told him, shifting her legs so that they were tucked up against him instead of locked behind his back.

Eric didn't immediately fall into a rhythm again. Instead, he sat back and looked at how she had arranged herself. "How about this?" Then, instead of tucking her knee under his arm—a position that worked well for her before—he instead tucked his arm behind her knee, lifting her leg over his shoulder. But just the one.

She felt her body tighten around him with this new angle and sucked in a quick breath. "Yeah," she said, adjusting to the different sensations. He felt larger, harder—and she felt closer to someone else than she'd been in so long. "Yeah, let's try that."

This time, his pace wasn't slow or measured. He wasn't taking his time, not anymore. This time, he buried himself inside of her over and over again and it couldn't have been more than a minute before her body tightened and the orgasm blazed through her. She cried out, "Eric!" And then she lost the ability to speak at all.

He didn't give her the chance to catch her breath. He didn't give her the time to come back down to earth from that beautiful orgasm. Instead, he drove her relentlessly, pushing her from that high peak to one even higher. This time, when she came, she thrashed against the bed, grabbed onto his shoulders and held tight. The cords of his neck stood out as he roared and then collapsed on her.

They were breathing heavily. She could still feel him inside of her, although he was already retreating.

She shifted, trying to hold on to him even though she knew he couldn't stay.

She didn't want to let him go. Not now. Maybe not ever.

But she did, of course. She had to. There were practical considerations and cold hard facts that could not be ignored. So when Eric rolled off her, withdrawing completely, she had no choice but to let him go.

Not that he went far. He pulled her into his arms, shaping himself around her and whispering "My beautiful, beautiful Sofia" into her hair, and that was it.

She loved him.

What a shame she could never have him.

Thirteen

It was hard to think with his pulse pounding in his ears and his body vibrating at a pitch Eric wasn't sure he'd ever heard before. But one thought pushed its way through the collection of purely physical reactions to making love with Sofia.

He was in *so* much trouble.

Because he'd promised Sofia they could have some fun this weekend. He could make her feel good. She could have a break from being a mother and a widow and be... Well, not his significant other, but a woman with wants and needs that he could meet. And above all else, he'd promised her that no matter what happened, they would always be friends. Friends with benefits, yes. But friends first.

He wasn't sure he could be anything as trite as

"just friends" with her ever again. Not after *that*. Jesus.

He hadn't had sex in over six months. Closer to ten, now that he thought about it. It was possible this wave of possessive emotion was nothing more than a long-standing itch finally being scratched. He'd gotten lucky again and it was a relief.

Sofia kissed the hollow of his neck. "I'll be right back," she said softly, pulling away from him.

He fought the urge to pull her right back into his arms. Stupid urges. Instead, all he could say was "Okay," as if that were some brilliant pillow talk. He watched her cross in front of the bed and disappear into his bathroom and then he dropped his head back against the pillows.

His blood was still pounding in his veins like a call to arms. He should be good now. Tired. Ready to sleep. An evening of sexual anticipation had paid off for both of them. Now he could stop thinking about Sofia.

Yeah, *right*. Because one thing was clear—bedding Sofia was not an itch that had been scratched. This was something else. What he'd felt with her wasn't just satisfaction at a job well done.

Oh, he was in so much trouble.

He wasn't an impulsive person. He *wasn't*. But ever since she'd shown up in his office and his life again, he'd been making impulsive decisions. He'd hired her without running background checks or calling her references. He'd taken her shopping because she'd been worried about what she would wear this weekend.

He'd bedded her. Twice. She was his office manager and he'd been inside of her. And, God help him, if she gave him so much as a half smile and a long look, he'd be inside of her again. He wasn't sure he could control himself.

When he'd pulled himself together in those months after discovering Prudence's son wasn't his, he'd been forced to make the adult, mature decision not to engage in any more casual sex. It scratched an itch but it never made him feel better, not in the long run. He'd needed something more in bed—and out of it.

This weekend was supposed to be casual. Just two friends helping each other out. Getting her back on her feet.

He dropped his head into his hands. God help him, nothing about this was casual. This was Sofia. He cared about her. And her children? Those two innocent little babies who didn't have a father and yet were so full of joy and laughter?

What was wrong with him? He was a thirty-one-year-old bachelor billionaire. The world was his playground. He could have anything he wanted. Anyone he wanted.

Why did he want Sofia? Not just a sexual relationship. He wanted it all. He wanted to be her family. A husband to her wife, a father to her children. He wanted the perfect ending to this story. He wanted the perfect life. One that he could only have with Sofia.

And dumbass that he was, he'd promised her that he could keep this casual. Just a weekend of letting off a little steam in between billion-dollar business negotiations.

He never should have hired her. He should have listened to his better instincts and immediately gotten her a good-paying job somewhere—anywhere— else and then asked her on a proper date. He'd been lying to himself from the very beginning about what he wanted from her.

He didn't want Sofia as his office manager. He wanted her as his everything.

He was the biggest idiot in the world.

Because he had promised. And trying to change the terms of the deal now could do more than just ruin the rest of his weekend. They worked together. She was still mourning her husband. She might never want to replace the father of her children. Not even with Eric.

The bathroom door opened and she walked out, her body on full display. She stood at the foot of the bed, her lips curved into a knowing smile as she looked down on him.

He was in *so* much damned trouble.

He had to get his head out of his ass. He got out of bed and kissed her. He could spend the rest of his life kissing her, he realized. Her warm body pressed against him and his body started to respond.

He stepped back. He wasn't some randy kid any-more, for God's sake. But there was no missing that blush high on Sofia's cheeks. "All right?"

She nodded. "I'm going to go get a few things from my room and check in with my mom."

"I'll be here." Once she was gone, Eric stared at his reflection in the mirror. He looked the same, but everything was different.

He liked sex. He'd always liked sex. But aside from maybe the first few times, where it was as if a whole new world had been opened up to him, he couldn't ever remember feeling this changed after making love with someone. Certainly not with his ex-fiancée. It hadn't been bad, sleeping with Pru-dence. They'd both enjoyed it. It just…

It hadn't left him a changed man. And he knew damned good and well that after Sofia, he'd never be the same again.

After he pulled on his shorts, he walked out to the kitchen and grabbed a sparkling water from the fridge. He never drank more than a glass or two of anything on a business trip. The last thing anyone needed was for him to get sloshed and torpedo a deal. So his rooms were always stocked with coffee, tea and sparkling water.

Frankly, he could use a drink right now. Some-thing to help him get this wash of confusion under control. Because he wanted everything about Sofia—and he had no idea how to get it. Not without send-ing her running for the hills.

Sofia came back into the room. She'd dressed in a tank top and a pair of panties—he thought. He was sorely tempted to lift the hem on the shirt and double-check. She didn't seem the least bit self-conscious about walking around like that and Eric didn't feel the least bit self-conscious staring at her.

"Mom sent a picture—do you want to see?" she asked.

"Of course." Those two adorable children were sitting in matching high chairs, looking like they'd rolled around in a plate of spaghetti. Sauce and noodles were everywhere and they were grinning the same huge smile. Strangely, it was everything he needed and salt in the wound at the same time because they weren't his babies.

Somehow, he managed to chuckle. "I bet bath time is hilarious at your house."

"You have no idea," she said, sounding like a battle-scarred veteran instead of a young mother.

He handed her the water. He should be saying things, he realized. Telling her how beautiful she was, how great the sex was. He'd never had any trouble coming up with those sorts of things before.

All of these easy words abandoned him. All he could say as he handed the phone back to her was, "Come to bed."

She looked up at him through her lashes and it took everything he had not to sweep her off her feet and make love to her all over again. "All right."

Hand in hand, they walked back to the bed. She

was wearing panties, but a different pair than earlier. These were hers, not the ones Clarice had picked out for her. He liked them all the better for that.

He pulled the covers up over them and turned off the light. He didn't know if he would be able to sleep, but he hoped she would.

Long dark minutes passed before she said, "Eric?"

"Yeah, babe?"

She didn't answer for second, just flattened her hand against his chest. "I just want you to know— this really means a lot to me. I…I've never been with anyone else but my husband. Never even shared a bed with anyone else."

He swallowed hard. "I'm honored."

With a sigh, she burrowed deeper into him. God, she felt good there, her weight against his side. "Thank you for holding me. For being here for me. You've no idea how much it means to me."

Her trust was a gift. He honestly wasn't sure he was worthy of it. "I will always be here for you, Sofia," he said, because it was as close to the truth as he could get without changing the terms of their deal.

Sleep was a long time coming.

Even though he was forty feet away and there were probably thirty people standing in between them, Eric had not been able to stop looking at Sofia all night long. She was on the other side of the Star-light Room, a ballroom at the top of the Chase Park Plaza, listening to a conversation between the city planner's assistant and the wife of the contractor Steve preferred to use for the demolition.

Tonight, Sofia was wearing a cocktail dress of red lace. She was gorgeous in it and the low lighting in the room—supposedly starlight—made her practically glow. She was simply gorgeous, he decided. And he loved her in red.

Maybe he should get her some red lingerie—something lacy and tantalizing. Maybe with matching stockings and a garter belt. And a pair of black high heels. The vision of Sofia made it difficult for Eric to stand upright. All day long, he'd struggled to focus on the deal at hand. The effort it took not to moon over her was harder than he'd expected it to be.

She needed a strand of black pearls looped around her neck, he decided. She hadn't let Clarice add any jewelry to the outfits. Pearls nestled between her breasts, matching earrings dangling…

"The vision for the space…" someone was saying to him, but he wasn't paying attention. How much longer until he could pull her away from here? Until he could strip her out of that dress and lay her on his bed? The hours since he'd made love to her this morning felt like a lifetime. He wouldn't be able to hold out much longer.

But just then, Sofia stepped away from her conversation. Eric had to crane his neck, but he saw that she was staring down at her phone.

Instantly he went on alert. Something was wrong. He didn't know how he knew, but he did. That feeling only got stronger when she walked toward the hallway outside the ballroom, her phone already at her ear.

Eric followed her. His first thought went to the kids. Were they all right?

"Mr. Jenner," the mayor said, pulling him aside. "Have you met…"

"Ladies and gentlemen," Eric said, smiling broadly. He didn't have time to be the billionaire businessman right now. Sofia needed him. "If you would excuse me for a moment, there's something I need to see to."

He managed to get the rest of the way across the room without being intercepted by anyone else who wanted to shake his hand and welcome him to St. Louis. The details of the deal still had to be ironed out, but it looked like this development was going to happen and everyone was in a celebratory mood.

Everyone except for Sofia. He was all but running by the time he burst through the doors and into the hall. When Sofia jerked around to look at him, his heart dropped. He knew that look. She was on the verge of a full-on panic attack. Dammit, he hated being right sometimes. He walked up to her and put his hands on her shoulders, willing her to be strong. "What's wrong?"

Her words cut him like a knife. "The twins are sick."

For a moment, he couldn't do anything but stare

down into her worried eyes as a feeling of complete and total helplessness swamped him. "How sick?"

He was not going to panic until he knew whether this was a case of the sniffles run amok or something more serious.

"Mom said they started throwing up last night. She…" Sofia's lips trembled and she clutched Eric's arm. "Dad rushed Eddy to the hospital a few minutes ago. He wasn't responding. Eric, what are we going to do?" That last part came out as a sob.

He tried to make sense of what she was saying—but he wasn't coming up with anything. "They were fine last night. Your mom sent that picture, didn't she? Spaghetti?"

Sofia was taking in huge gulps of air, but for all that, Eric wasn't sure she was actually breathing. "She said Miss Rita was sick. And she didn't want to worry me today because I was working and I was supposed to be having fun. She said she kept hoping that the kids would work it out of their systems today, but Eddy kept getting worse and worse and Addy isn't much better and my baby is in the hospital and I'm in St. Louis! They need me and I'm not there!"

He didn't know anything about sick kids or hospitals but he knew that Sofia having a panic attack wouldn't help anyone right now. He had to keep her calm and get her moving. "I'm going to get you there," he promised. "We're leaving. Now."

The color left her face. "But your deal…"

He grabbed her hand and hauled her back into

the hotel ballroom until he found Meryl and Steve. "Sofia's kids are sick," he said without any other introductions. "We're leaving. I want you guys to stay, make my apologies. I don't care how you get home. You can rent a car, take the train—charge it to the company credit card. I can send the plane back for you—"

"That won't be necessary," Steve said quickly.

"Go," Meryl said, giving Sofia a hug. "Take care of your kids. We've got this."

Sofia let out a little sob. Eric hooked her arm with his and guided her away from the party. While they waited for the elevator, he called his pilot and said, "I don't care how you do it, but we need to be in the air in an hour. If not sooner. Make it happen."

Finally, after what felt like a year, the elevator dinged and the doors opened. "It's going to be okay, babe," he said again as he guided Sofia into the elevator. Once the doors closed, he wrapped his arms around her shoulders and held her tight. She clung to him and it just about killed him. She was so worried and he couldn't snap his fingers and make it better.

All he could do was the next best thing. He could get her to her babies a hell of a lot faster than anyone else could. He could make sure Eddy had the very best care. And, God forbid, if anything happened, he'd be there for her. Because that's what friends were for.

But that wasn't true and he knew it. Because what he felt for Sofia went well beyond "friends" or even friends with benefits. What he felt for her wasn't casual and it wasn't friendly. She'd ignited a passion in his heart that he'd been missing for months. Years. Because he hadn't felt this way about Prudence. He hadn't fought for her.

But Sofia? Eddy and Addy? By God, he was going to fight for them. The truth hit him with a lurch.

Sofia and her children were his family. And he'd do anything for them.

And that started now.

He rubbed her back and said, "We'll be there in a few hours. Everything's going to be fine," in his most reassuring voice.

She began to cry and all he could do was hold her. "I'm sorry," she blubbered, trying to get herself under control and, in Eric's opinion, failing miserably. "It's just that when David died…"

He crushed her to his chest. "That's not what's happening here," he said, even though he knew it wasn't a promise he could make. "Eddy's going to be fine. He's a tough little dude." He prayed. "Did your mom say where he was?"

"St. Anthony."

Dammit, he didn't know anyone there, at least not off the top of his head. If they could get Eddy to the Children's Hospital, then he knew some of the staff there. He donated a lot of money to the Children's Hospital.

Then it hit him—Robert Wyatt. The man was a doctor and the scion of the Wyatt Pharmaceuticals empire. Even if Wyatt didn't treat children—Eric wanted to think the man was a surgeon?—he'd be able to recommend the best for Eddy.

Normally Eric would never call in this favor. He had a friendly rivalry with Marcus Warren—but there was nothing friendly about his rivalry with Wyatt. The only reason the two men hadn't come to blows was that they were in different industries and even then, there'd been that one time…

No, he absolutely shouldn't call in this favor. But then Sofia looked up at him, tears in her eyes and he knew he had to. Eric would do anything he could to make Eddy better—even bring in Wyatt.

"I'll make some calls," he said. Wyatt wouldn't exactly jump at the chance to help Eric out, but frankly, he wasn't going to take no for an answer. The man owed him.

Sofia nodded tearfully and made a visible effort to pull herself together. Just then, the elevator slowed and the doors opened. "Let's go," she said, her jaw set.

They all but ran to their rooms. It took less than five minutes for them to grab their things and then they were running for the elevator again. Neither of them wasted time changing out of their party clothes. Eric stopped shoving his clothes into his bag only long enough to call down to the front desk and tell them to have a car ready to leave for the airport immediately. Any car would do.

He had to get Sofia to her son. Now.

Fourteen

Sofia hadn't noticed the landing. She couldn't have said if it was rough or smooth or perfect or a near-disaster. All she could think about was her children.

"Well?" Eric said when she hung up with her mom.

Sofia took a steadying breath, but it didn't steady anything. Eric's driver whipped the car around corners and ran red lights in true Chicago fashion and not even the seat belts could keep her from sliding all over the place. "She's home with Addy. She said Addy's drinking fluids from a bottle, which is good. She hasn't thrown up in two hours."

"Good," Eric said encouragingly, rubbing his thumb along the side of her hand. He hadn't let go of her since…well, since they'd gotten into the elevator to leave the hotel. She might not remember much about the flight or the middle-of-the-night landing, but she knew that Eric had been there.

Like he was right now. "And your dad's still at the hospital with Eddy?"

She nodded, her head feeling like lead. It was three in the morning and panic was exhausting. If it weren't for Eric, she had no idea how she would have made it.

"We're almost there," he said, all reassuring confidence. God, how she wished she could be reassured right now.

But she couldn't. All she could do was stare out the windows as familiar Chicago streets whipped by.

If she hadn't gone to St. Louis, then she would've been there when her babies got sick. She could've comforted them—and gotten them to the doctor sooner, at the very least. Her parents generally refused to go to the doctor unless things were dire because they didn't want to waste money on something like a cold.

She hadn't explained that to Eric because she wasn't sure he'd understand. But the fact that her parents had decided to take Eddy to the emergency room terrified Sofia because it meant something was really wrong with her baby.

God, she should have been here for her children. And instead, what had she been doing?

Sleeping with Eric.

For the first time since David's death, she had

been a little bit selfish. She'd put herself first instead of putting her children first. And now?

Now she was racing to a hospital, hoping like hell she wasn't too late.

She was going to be ill. That's all there was to it. Because this was too familiar, this late-night mad dash to the hospital, hoping that she'd get there in time. Hoping no one would die.

"I found David," she heard herself say.

She didn't want to relive the worst day of her life, but the horrifying thought that it might not have been the worst day had her talking. "He got up. In the middle of the night. He'd had a headache all afternoon and it was getting worse, so he was going to take something. I was so pregnant I couldn't sleep so when he didn't come back to bed, I went looking for him. He was crumpled in the middle of the kitchen floor."

Eric lifted her hand to his mouth. "What happened?"

"They said it was an aneurysm. He…" Her breath caught in her throat. Would this ever get easier? "He was gone by the time they got him to the hospital. It was the worst day of my life."

"Oh, babe." Undoing his seat belt, Eric scooted over to her and wrapped his arms around her. "This isn't the same. Eddy's sick but he's not going to die. Not if I have anything to say about it."

"You don't," she said, willing herself to be numb. She couldn't take any more pain. *Please*, she thought, *please don't let* this *be the worst day of my life.* "No one does."

"Sofia." His tone was more commanding now and, when he cupped her cheek in the palm of his hand, she had no choice but to look him in the eye. Even in the dark car, she could see a fierceness to him that she hadn't seen before. "This isn't your fault."

Of course she knew that. But her eyes watered anyway as she said, "I should have been here, Eric. I should have been with my kids when they were sick instead..."

Instead of being with you.

She didn't say it out loud.

She didn't have to.

Something in Eric's eyes shifted and he looked like he might cry. Which was ridiculous. Why would he be upset over a sick kid? She was overreacting, of course. Mom guilt was a thing.

But Eric had no claims to her or her kids. They were friends, yeah—friends with some benefits, at least. She'd pulled him away from a huge business deal, though. She was putting his business at risk. And for what?

Before she could finish that thought, the car came to a screeching halt. Eric pulled away from her as she looked dumbly out the window. They were in front of the hospital.

"Let's go."

He helped her out of the car and then held on to her hand as they ran inside. "Which floor?"

"Third."

When the elevator doors closed behind them, Eric turned to her and cupped her face. "Take a deep breath, Sofia," he said, his voice somewhere between soothing and commanding. Eric stroked her cheeks with his thumb. "In and out. Panic is contagious and we don't want to upset him, do we?"

Her lungs—she wasn't sure they'd worked right in hours. But she forced herself to breathe. It was a struggle, but Eric was right. If she rolled into that room hysterical and sobbing, it would only agitate Eddy. "I'm so sorry about the deal."

This was exactly what she'd been afraid of—somehow, she'd ruin the deal and show him why it was a mistake to pretend she fit by his side.

God, what a mess.

"Sofia," he said, laughter in his voice. "How could you think the deal means anything to me when you need me? When Eddy needs me? You and your children are so much more to me than that."

Sofia's breath caught in her throat. In any other circumstances, that would have been a statement so romantic it was practically a declaration. She mentally shook her head, though. He was just trying to make her feel better. Lord knew she needed all the help she could get right now.

The elevator dinged and they were on the pediatric floor. It took some doing but they found the right room and there was her father, sitting in the chair, looking tired and old. "Sofia," he said, coming to his feet and pulling her into a hug that threatened to undo her all over again. "Everything is fine. He's responding well but they're keeping him sedated so he doesn't pull out the IV. And there can only be one…"

She didn't hear what her father was saying as she collapsed in the chair next to Eddy's bed. The lump in her throat was huge and she was having trouble breathing again.

"There's my serious little man," Eric said, stepping around her. She saw him pull the blanket up and realized that he was covering the IV port in Eddy's arm so she wouldn't have to see it. Then she watched him smooth her baby's hair away from his tiny little face. Even though he was unconscious, Eddy's lips twitched into something that looked so much like a smile that it almost broke her heart.

Eric looked at her and she remembered she was supposed to be breathing. She held Eddy's little hand in hers and said, "Mommy's here, baby. Sorry it took so long, but I'm here now and you are doing such a good job."

She was aware of Eric squeezing her shoulder, aware that her father was saying something to her. She nodded, even though she didn't catch what he'd said. The room got quiet, except for the beeping of the machines and the roaring sound of her guilt.

Time lost all meaning as she watched his little

chest rise and fall. Her son wore nothing but a diaper and he looked so small. So helpless.

She should have been here for him, not in Eric's bed. She'd let her baby down and for what? If something happened to Eddy, she didn't know how she'd ever forgive herself.

"Good morning," a deep male voice rumbled from the doorway. "Ms. Bingham, correct?"

Sofia startled and hurriedly wiped tears away from her face. When she looked at the doctor, she startled again. "Wyatt? Robert Wyatt?"

Because it sure as hell looked like the boy who'd tried to cop a feel twenty years ago—except all grown up. The man before her was tall and broad, with dashing dark hair and bright blue eyes.

And a white lab coat with a stethoscope hanging out of his pocket.

What was going on?

"Dr. Wyatt, actually. Do I know you?" he said, staring at her. "Wait…"

She scrubbed at her face. How could this day get any stranger? The last person she wanted to see was Robert Wyatt—especially when she was a mess. "I'm sorry. I'm Sofia. I was a friend of Eric's, back when we were kids."

His eyes bulged in his head. "You're the maid's daughter, right?"

Embarrassment flashed down the back of her neck. Even after all this time, she was still the maid's daughter. This weekend it'd been fun to pretend she could live in Eric's world, but it was just that—pretend. Eric might not realize the truth but everyone else? All the other people who fit naturally into his world?

She'd always be *just* the maid's daughter. She'd be a liability to him.

She eyed Wyatt, wondering if she should kick him again. But Wyatt beat her to the punch. "I owe you an apology, then."

She was so surprised at that statement that all she could do was blink. "What?"

And Wyatt blushed. He blushed! Because of her! What the hell was going on? "Look, I know it was a long time ago and we were just kids and you probably don't even remember it—"

"I remember you cornered me," she said quietly.

He looked pained. "Like I said, I owe you an apology. What I did was wrong. I shouldn't have tried to grab you. Although," he added, shooting her a sheepish smile, "if I recall correctly, you got your revenge."

This was the weirdest conversation she'd ever had. "This is all very well and good, but why are you here?" Because she didn't want to rehash old memories with a boy she'd never liked. She just wanted her son to get better.

He looked at her in surprise. "Jenner called me. He said a friend's baby was sick and he asked me to check things over. I just didn't realize you were the friend in question." As he spoke, he headed toward the computer terminal and logged in.

"Excuse me," she said again, her head feeling heavy. "But are you even qualified to be in this room?"

"Hmm," he said, looking over the file. Then he answered her question. "In addition to Wyatt Pharmaceuticals, I'm a pediatric surgeon. That's why Jenner called me. Well," he added, shooting a quick smile in her direction, "that and I owed him one. Or, more specifically, I owed you one, so I guess I still owe him one." He chuckled. Sofia blinked, trying to follow that train of thought. Nope. She was still at the station.

"Now, about your son. Has anyone talked to you yet?" Wyatt asked. She shook her head slowly. "There has been a particularly nasty strain of the stomach flu going around. It hits hard but doesn't last long. He's responding well to treatment." He moved to Eddy's bedside, lightly touching his little body. "He's going to be fine," Wyatt said sympathetically. "There wasn't anything anyone could have done differently."

Now that was exactly the sort of bull line that was condescending and irritating. Of course she could have done things differently! She could have stayed home and taken care of her kids like she was supposed to and, in the process, not doomed Eric's deal! She could have made sure that things hadn't gotten to the point where *Wyatt* was offering her false platitudes of comfort!

"I never liked you," she blurted out and then, mortified, she added, "I'm sorry. I haven't slept and I'm very worried."

Wyatt snorted. He didn't even look offended. "I had that coming. But you don't have to like me. You just have to trust me when I say that your son is going to make a full and—knowing kids—*fast* recovery. I'll confer with the resident on duty before I leave but I'd be willing to bet he goes home tomorrow."

Sofia tried to say something, but her words got blocked up in her throat as she stared down at Eddy. *Please, please let Wyatt be right.*

"Thank you for coming," she finally got out. "I appreciate it."

Wyatt didn't reply for a long moment, which made her look up at him. "Thank you for accepting my apology. I must say, Jenner doesn't call in favors for just anyone." His smile warmed. "But I can see why he did. Take care, Sofia."

And just like that, he was gone.

Sofia sat there in a state of shock for a long time. Alone. What the heck had Wyatt meant when he'd said he could see why Eric had called in a favor?

She wished Eric were here. She wanted him right then. He had risked so much for her. It didn't make any sense because he was a billionaire and powerful and sexy and freaking great in bed and wonderful with her kids and apparently stupid enough to put huge deals in danger just for...

For *her*?

Idiot man.

She wanted to apologize for costing him the deal and making him waste his favors on her but she also wanted to bury her face against his chest and have him tell her it would be all right.

Hell, she didn't know what she wanted. Not anymore. She'd gone into this wanting a good job to take care of her family. Nothing more.

But even that was a lie. Because she could have applied for any number of jobs. Instead, she'd shot for the moon. And why?

Because of Eric. Because she'd wanted something more. And for a glorious day and a half, she'd had it. He'd made her feel things, *want* things that she'd forgotten she'd even dreamed of. Love. Satisfaction.

Happiness.

For the first time since her husband had died, Sofia had dared to be a little selfish. And what had it gotten her?

Eddy was hooked up to an IV in the hospital. Addy was also sick at home and Sofia couldn't even be there for her daughter because she was with Eddy. She might have done permanent damage to Eric's business.

And Eric wasn't here. Sofia wasn't sure she'd ever felt so alone.

Where was he?

Fifteen

By the time Eddy woke up, hungry and cranky and so perfectly normal that Sofia could barely hold it together, her mom had shown up at the hospital. Sofia did manage to ask how Addy was doing, to which her mother replied, "Much better. She's been sleeping and—" but that was when the nurse and the doctor came in and began unhooking Eddy from his IV and Sofia didn't get to finish her conversation with her mother.

She knew she looked like hell and felt worse. She'd managed to snatch a few hours of broken rest after Wyatt's mysterious appearance, but nobody slept well in a hospital, least of all a worried mother.

By the time Sofia and Mom left with Eddy, it was two in the afternoon and Sofia was still wearing the same pair of shapewear she'd had on for the last thirty-some-odd hours. Her dress was no longer pretty but wilted and wrinkled, just like Sofia.

The funny thing was that they didn't take a cab home. Eric's car and driver were waiting for them, complete with a car seat for Eddy in the back. It was the sort of thoughtful gesture that made Sofia realize she couldn't be upset with Eric. He might have disappeared at some point in the middle of the night, but it was thoughtful of him to send the car. Besides, it wasn't like she expected him to hang out in the hospital waiting room. There hadn't been space for him in Eddy's small room and he wasn't the boy's father.

She had no idea what was going to happen at work tomorrow. Or even if she was going to work tomorrow. How was she supposed to do her job now that she and Eric had fallen into bed together? Would she even be able to walk into his office without thinking of him moving over her? Or would he conveniently "find" another job for her, one that removed her from the office, like he'd done for the last employee who'd tried to seduce him? And sleeping with him didn't even count the damage she might have done to his deal. If he lost the St. Louis development, would he blame her? Her stomach turned at the thought.

It'd been a mistake, she'd realized at some point in the middle of the night. She never should've mixed business and pleasure. It had been a mistake to leave her children for the weekend and that mistake had been compounded by sleeping with Eric.

He would be upset, she knew. But the plain truth was that she did not have the time or energy to start a relationship. Her children had to come first and Eric was a bachelor. A gorgeous billionaire bachelor. Frankly, she'd never figured out why he was interested in her in the first place. Not when he could have his pick of anyone—and they both knew he could. He was the very highest of the high and she was...

Well, she was more than just the maid's daughter. But she was a single mom, an office manager. She didn't fit with him. That's all there was to it.

Still, she thought as she sank back into the luxurious leather seating of Eric's car, being with Eric had been a gift in and of itself. A misguided one, but still. She had not died when her husband had. She had struggled and mourned, but she hadn't given up and she still had the capacity to open her heart to someone else. She still needed love. She still wanted to share her heart—and her body—with someone.

It just couldn't be Eric. A weekend's wardrobe of couture clothing didn't change the differences between them. Billionaire bachelors didn't get involved with widowed office managers with twin toddlers. They didn't deal with dirty diapers and barfing and the constant messes and sleepless nights. They jetted around the country with supermodels on their arms and partied with the rich and famous.

Her head hurt just thinking about Eric in the arms of another woman, which was, again, not logical. She couldn't have him and she had no right to be jealous of someone else having him.

Eddy fussed mightily as they pulled up in front of the house and Sofia unbuckled him. She was suddenly desperate to see Addy. It wasn't fair to her daughter that she hadn't been able to get home and see her yet.

Sofia followed her mom inside, dragging hard. She needed to change and she couldn't remember the last time she ate something. But she had to see her baby girl first. "Addy? Honey, Mommy's home," she called out softly.

"She's in the living room," Mom said as she headed for the kitchen. "With—"

Sofia came to a stumbling halt as she turned the corner. Because Addy was, indeed, in the living room—fast asleep on Eric's chest. Eric was sprawled out on the ancient family couch. He'd lost both his jacket and his button-up shirt at some point and was wearing nothing but a T-shirt that, even at this distance, Sofia could see was stained. Addy had a blanket draped around her, and Eric was holding her, one hand under her bottom, the other across her back.

Oh, God. Had he been here with her daughter the entire night?

She must've gasped or something because just then, Eric's eyes fluttered open. He blinked and then focused on her. "Hey," he said, smiling sleepily. "You guys are home. That's wonderful. Addy and I have been holding down the couch for you."

And it wasn't fair, damn it all, that he was here with Addy while she had been at the hospital with Eddy. It wasn't fair that, even in a stained T-shirt, he was still the most handsome man she'd ever seen. And it wasn't fair that, just when she'd realized she could never be right for him, he went and made her fall in love with him all over again.

"How long have you been here?"

"What time is it?" he asked, stretching carefully so that he didn't jostle the baby girl.

"Two thirty." It was naptime, she realized. Eric and Addy had been napping together and it was so perfectly sweet it was going to break her heart.

He yawned. "I think I left the hospital a little before four? Addy was pretty fussy, but she seemed calmer when I held her, so I stayed. Sorry I didn't get back to check on you and Eddy. How are you doing, big guy?" he asked when Eddy swiveled his head around at the sound of his name.

At the same time, Addy jolted awake. She looked up and saw Sofia. Instantly, her lips began to quiver.

Eric sat up and kissed Addy's head and it wasn't fair because Sofia wanted him so much and it simply wouldn't work. There were reasons she couldn't have this. Good reasons. That she couldn't think of right now.

Eric stood and came toward her and her breath caught in her throat. "Trade you," he said, as Addy leaned toward Sofia and Eddy pitched toward Eric because even her son was happy to see him. Eric caught the little boy in his arms and Sofia knew she wasn't imagining that the man was happy to see her baby boy.

She caught Addy in her arms and hugged the little girl to her chest, trying to find her balance. But before that happened, Eric leaned over and kissed Sofia's forehead. "I'm so glad you're home, babe. I hated leaving you there, but I figured you'd want me to be with Addy."

"I…" She blinked at him. His jaw was scruffy and he was rumpled and he was still the sexiest man she'd ever seen.

"Listen," Eric said, his voice low as he rubbed Eddy's back. "I was thinking—your parents are great, but this is a super small house and the kids need room to grow. My dad was touring a condo on the Gold Coast that would be perfect for us."

"Us?" He hadn't said *us*, had he? No, she was just hearing things. She was tired and—

"Three thousand square feet, a great view of the lake—plenty of room for the kids. Closer to everything. And we could get a better couch," he joked, stretching like a cat.

"Eric…" Maybe she was still dreaming. She'd fallen asleep in the hospital and was hallucinating that a man like Eric Jenner had spent the last God-only-knew-how-many hours taking care of a sick baby.

And waiting on her. Waiting to—to what? To ask

her to move in with him? Or just… "I can't afford a Gold Coast condo, Eric."

He had the nerve to snort in amusement. "I wouldn't expect you to split the cost with me, babe. It's a gift for you. For us."

There was that word again. *Us.* And Eric was saying it while soothing a clingy Eddy.

But Sofia was not feeling calm. "What are you talking about? Because it sounds like…" Like he wanted her to move her whole family in with him. How did that make any sense?

It didn't.

"Not today, of course," he said, completely oblivious to her confusion. "The condo needs to be remodeled. But I can buy it and when it's ready, we can move in together."

Her mouth flopped open. She wasn't dreaming this, was she? He was asking her to move in with him.

"I'd hope," he went on, stepping in closer and shifting so he could cup her cheek in his palm without disrupting Eddy, "that you'd consider getting married before that point, though. I'll take you any way I can get you, but if you'll have me, I'd consider it the greatest honor of my life if you'd marry me, Sofia. I promised I'd take care of you and I meant it. For the rest of our lives, let me take care of you."

His thumb stroked over her cheek and Addy sighed in what felt like happiness and Eddy smiled at her from where he was tucked against Eric's chest and Sofia almost, *almost* said yes. This was every fantasy come to life—a hot, rich, single billionaire who liked small children and was great in bed and was promising to give her the world on a silver platter.

But when she opened her mouth, *yes* wasn't what came out. Because she did love him and she did want him and her babies loved him…but how on earth could he think she could fit into his world?

How much would it cost him if she said yes? Not just this deal. There was always something with kids.

She couldn't do this to him. She couldn't saddle him with her life, her problems, couldn't expect him to step into the role of father to someone else's children.

Oh, this hurt. But it was the right thing to do. He'd see that soon enough.

"Eric, no."

Sixteen

Eric stared down in confusion at Sofia, who was clutching Addy to her chest as if the toddler was a shield. "No *what*?"

Because it seemed like there should be an additional thought there. No, she didn't like the Gold Coast. No, she didn't want to wait to get married.

Not *no thank you*. She couldn't mean that. He forged ahead. "We don't have to live on the Gold Coast. We can look around. I want you to be happy with whatever place we choose."

Her eyes bugged out of her head and she stepped away from him. Eric had no choice but to let his hand fall away. "Eric, *no*," she repeated with more force. "I can't marry you. What the hell—heck," she quickly corrected, glancing at her children, "are you even thinking, talking like this?"

He could understand that she was upset. It had been an upsetting couple of days. But this was different.

"I was thinking I care for you. And your children. I was thinking…" He swallowed nervously as her eyes opened even wider. "I was thinking we could be a family."

All the blood drained out of her face and he wasn't sure she was breathing. She took another jerky step away from him before he could wrap his free arm around her.

"I can't do this, Eric," she said, her voice breaking. "What happened this weekend… I can't. When they needed me I wasn't here. I was with you and it was fine when we were alone but I don't know how to live in your world and I don't want to damage your business and…"

"What are you talking about?"

She swallowed hard a couple of times, squeezing her eyes shut. That didn't stop the tears from trickling down her cheeks. "I can't be with you. I have to put my children first. Always."

He opened his mouth, closed it and then tried again. How did that make any sense? It didn't. He wasn't trying to get rid of her kids. He loved these babies. He wanted to give her children a father. He wanted to be her husband. "Babe, you're tired. You're upset. You're not thinking clearly right—"

He knew the moment the words left his mouth that they were wrong. Her eyes flashed with anger and she reached out and plucked Eddy from his chest. Even though he'd known the babies such a short time, Eric felt almost lost without a twin in his arms. "I *am* thinking clearly, Eric. What happened this weekend risked everything. I shouldn't have left my kids. I shouldn't have been with you. I shouldn't have been so stupid, so damned selfish."

"Sofia," he managed to get out. "Slow down. Kids get sick, don't they? And you didn't cost me a deal. I promise you—even if it falls through, it's not going to bankrupt me."

She stared at him and then barked out a bitter laugh. "No, of course not. Of course you could afford to lose a deal this huge. Don't you see, Eric? I don't fit in your world. How could I? I'm just the office manager. The maid's daughter. A widowed single mom. I'll never belong and every time you try to make me fit, something bad will happen." She choked out a rough sob. "And I can't let anything else bad happen. I couldn't take it if something bad happened to you."

Both babies began to cry and her parents appeared in the doorway behind her, looking frantic.

"Sofia," he said softly, holding up his hands in the universal sign of surrender. "You do fit. I thought this weekend proved that."

"Oh, please," she said and he honestly couldn't tell if she was being sarcastic or if she was begging him.

Timing was everything, however, and there was no mistaking that his timing sucked. She was still in her cocktail dress and she probably hadn't slept and she'd been in a state of constant panic for the last day. "We can talk about this after you've gotten some—"

But she cut him off. "No, Eric—we can't. I…" She swallowed, apparently realizing they had an audience. She turned and handed the fussing babies over to her folks. "Can you give us a minute?" When her parents didn't move except to exchange worried glances, Sofia added "Please?" with more force.

"We'll be in the kitchen if you need us," her father said. Then he shot a look that Eric hoped was encouraging over Sofia's head.

Sofia glared at Eric until her parents were gone. And all he could do was stare back at her in surprise. "Babe," he began again, but she cut him off.

"No, Eric. I don't know what you're thinking, but *no*."

"I care for you," he got out before she could launch into another denial. "That's what I'm thinking. And I thought that, after what we shared this weekend, you cared for me, too."

Her throat worked and he got the feeling she was trying not to cry. "Damn you," she whispered, her voice hoarse. "Of course I do. Of course I care for you."

"Then why won't you let me take care of you?"

"You really think it's that easy? That you just snap your fingers and the world falls all over itself to meet your high expectations?" She snapped for emphasis. "That I meet your high expectations? For God's sake, Eric—look at me! I live with my parents because I can barely function on my own! I'm struggling to put one foot in front of the other!" She choked on the words again, curling into herself.

It about broke his heart because she wouldn't see reason. How was he supposed to comfort her if she wouldn't even let him touch her?

"Sofia," he said quietly. "What did Wyatt say to you?" Because yeah, she'd been worried about his deal before he'd left her at the hospital—but she hadn't been this frantic. And Eddy was doing so much better—so where was the disconnect?

It had to be Wyatt. Damn that man.

"He didn't say anything, Eric—except to tell me that Eddy would be fine." Her eyes were shiny and her voice wobbled as she spoke. "But don't you see? You're a man who can fly me home at a moment's notice and call in favors from the heads of pharmaceutical companies and—"

"To make sure you're okay? And your kids are okay? You're damn right I'm going to do that—that and more," he cut in, trying not to yell. The maddening woman wasn't making any sense!

Which only made her look sadder. "But that's not my world, Eric."

"I don't care." Yeah, he was yelling. "I wouldn't care if you lived in a box! You're beautiful and intelligent and the bravest woman I've ever met! And

I…" His throat caught but he pushed on. "You were my best friend when we were kids and that hasn't changed. I still love you—but now I love you more. And for the life of me, I can't figure out why that makes me the bad guy here!"

She began to shake and he tried to pull her into his arms and make sure she was all right. But she moved—away from him. "I think you need to leave."

"Babe," he said, his voice gruff. "It never mattered to me. How different our lives have been."

But again, she dodged his grasp, turning and all but fleeing from the room. "It matters," he heard her mutter. In seconds, she was gone.

He heard a door slam from somewhere deeper in the house and then her father was back, looking apologetic. "Eric, I am sorry. It's been a long weekend and she's upset and…"

"I know." Eric scrubbed at the back of his neck. "My timing was crap. I was just so glad to see her and Eddy, you know?"

Emilio nodded. "I understand." He held out Eric's shirt and jacket. "I, ah, I do not think she will be in tomorrow."

The way the older man said it made Eric's stomach drop. "Of course not," he quickly agreed. "She's worn ragged and she'll want to make sure the kids are fully on the mend." He shrugged into his jacket. "But tell her I hope to see her on Tuesday, okay?"

Emilio nodded, but he didn't look convinced and Eric's stomach dropped another two notches.

He'd just found Sofia and her family.

He wasn't going to walk away from them all.

Sofia didn't come to work on Monday, which Eric expected. She also didn't show on Tuesday. "Her son was released from the hospital," he told Meryl and Steve when they came in to work on Tuesday. Sofia wasn't the only one who needed to recover from the weekend.

"Thank goodness for that," Steve said.

"Let us know if there's anything we can do to help," Meryl added.

But Eric just nodded and smiled and, when he got back to his desk, ordered two dozen roses delivered to Sofia's house.

She didn't come to work on Wednesday, either.

By Thursday, he was feeling frantic. Where was she? She hadn't quit. He was pretty sure he'd remember that. And it wasn't like Sofia to hide. Back when they'd been kids...

Eric slumped behind his desk. They weren't kids anymore. They couldn't go back to that easy friendship. He couldn't be just friends with her anymore. Or even friends with benefits.

He wanted to be with her through good and bad. He wanted to see her children grow up. He wanted children of his own. God, to see Sofia's body change and grow with his child—the longing was physically painful.

He wanted everything. With her—only with her—he could have it.

By God, he was Eric Jenner.

He was going to get it.

Seventeen

They didn't talk about the business trip. Or Eric. Or about the fact that Sofia hadn't gone back to work.

Suddenly, Sofia's household was quiet and tense, everyone walking around on eggshells. And, after Tuesday, they couldn't even hide behind the lie that it was because the twins were sick because they weren't. Dr. Robert Wyatt had been correct—Eddy and Addy bounced back as if they'd never been sick at all.

And Sofia couldn't even say she was moving through life in a fog—certainly not like she'd been after David died. She was tired, of course. It'd been a rough week. But sorrow wasn't the overarching emotion that kept her awake at night.

No, it was anger. Clear, bright anger that burned without flickering.

How dare Eric propose marriage just like *that*? What gave him the right to talk about love and marriage and condos, as if he could wave a magic wand and make everything perfect? Why couldn't he see that she didn't belong with him? All this talk of love was great but she wasn't a girl anymore. There was no avoiding the realities of her life. What would happen if she said yes? If she let herself get swept away? She'd spend the rest of her life trying to prove she belonged with him. Had she thought that dinner with the lieutenant governor or the cocktail party was draining? Ha! She'd have to achieve that level of acting every second of every day just to keep people like Dr. Robert Wyatt from sneering at her. And honestly, even if she did everything right and was the model wife—which wasn't going to happen in this life or the next—they'd still sneer.

The only person who didn't seem to realize this was Eric. Idiot man.

She got mad all over again every time she walked past the bouquet of flowers in the middle of the dining room table. Because those flowers were hard to miss. Two dozen of the biggest, reddest roses she'd ever seen—the house smelled like a florist's shop. It was ridiculous.

The anger burned for days.

She tried to forget it, though. Addy and Eddy were okay. Better than okay. They spent long afternoons at the park, the twins toddling all over. They didn't understand that the reason they got all this extra Mom time was that Sofia couldn't bring herself to go back to work. How was she supposed to face Eric?

When they made it home for lunch and then naptime, Sofia collapsed on the couch. She couldn't continue to ignore Eric in the hopes that he'd go away. The roses screamed loud and clear that they weren't done.

Five long days had passed since she'd brought Eddy home from the hospital and told Eric to leave. Five days since he'd told her he loved her and she'd—what? Told him it wouldn't work?

She was right. She lived in a cramped three-bedroom house with her parents. She was sitting on the same sofa she'd sat on her entire life. She didn't fit with him. In all honesty, she'd barely fit with David.

David hadn't died on purpose. Just like Miss Rita hadn't gotten the kids sick on purpose. Bad things happened.

She just wanted bad things to stop happening to *her*.

She dropped her head into her hands. Eric had been a good thing. A wonderful, amazing, fun thing. He'd made her feel safe and happy and…

And loved.

He'd made love to her and protected her and she…

God, she'd fallen completely in love with him. She'd always cared for him—but the dratted man was right. They weren't kids anymore and what she felt for him wasn't anything so simple as friendship.

And he'd said he loved her, too. He loved her and she loved him and he wanted to marry her and she'd—what? Said *no*?

That was the whole problem, wasn't it?

There was a quiet knock on the front door, which made Sofia startle. She threw herself off the couch before the visitor could ring the doorbell and wake up the twins.

She gasped when she looked through the glass, because there was Eric. Her first thought was, *Shouldn't he be on the water?* It was a beautiful Friday afternoon, after all.

She opened the door cautiously. "Eric? What are you doing here?"

The look of relief on his face when he saw her almost took her breath away. "Sofia," he said and just the sound of her name on his lips was almost enough to undo her. "I need to talk to you."

"Why?"

He gave her a look, one so familiar and comfortable that she smiled in spite of herself. "You know, when we were kids and we'd have a fight, your mom always had us apologize and make up."

"True." They hadn't argued much, but all children bickered. "But we're not kids anymore."

"No, we're not."

"Is that Eric?" Mom appeared behind Sofia, all but shoving her out of the house. "I'll keep an eye on the kids. Go on, now." The way she said it made Sofia instantly suspicious.

"What's going on?" But that was as far as she got before Mom shoved Sofia's purse into her hands and closed the door behind her. Sofia turned to glare at Eric, who didn't even have the decency to look guilty. "What did you do?"

"Your mom wants us to make up," he said, tucking her hand into the crook of his arm and leading her down the steps. His car was waiting. "You know, it's true—the more things change, the more they stay the same."

She came to a stop. "Eric…"

"I hope you've gotten some rest," he went on, as if small talk was why he was here when they both knew it wasn't. "I've been worried sick about you."

"You can't say things like that," she scolded gently. But even as she said it, her heart felt like it was going to break again.

He'd been worried about her. He'd done everything in his power to take care of her babies. He'd said he loved her.

And, fool that she was, she loved him back. Hopelessly.

"Listen, you stubborn woman," he began, but he was smiling as he said it.

"Great start, that," she muttered.

He cut her a look and she closed her mouth. "I don't think we can be friends anymore."

Her breath froze in her lungs, despite the summer heat. "What?" Because of all the things she'd thought he might say right then, that hadn't even made the list.

"Because I wasn't a very good friend," he went on. "I guess I was an out-of-sight, out-of-mind person. I left home and grew up and wasn't there for you, good times or bad."

She suddenly had to swallow several times. "Don't do this, Eric. It won't end well."

"Don't do what? Tell you I love you? Ask you to marry me again? Try to do it better than I did last time, when we were both exhausted and frantic?"

"You can't be with me," she reminded him.

"I'm Eric Jenner," he said, sounding cocky and imperious. "I can do whatever the hell I want because who's going to stop me? If I want to spend every afternoon aboard my boat, who'll say no? If I want to build luxury condos on the moon, all I have to do is snap my fingers and the best, brightest minds will make it happen. If I want to walk around in a duck outfit—"

"A duck outfit?" she gasped.

"I'd set off a new feathered fashion craze," he went on, ignoring her. "And if I want to fall in love with my office manager and her twin babies, who'd dare tell me it's a bad idea? You? I hope not, Sofia. Because you're smarter than that."

Oh, Lord. He wasn't really going to do this on the sidewalk, was he? "But others will."

He had the nerve to look dangerous. And dang it

all if it didn't send a thrill down her spine. "I can't stop them," he said, his voice low. Another part of her heart broke. "But if anyone dares insult you? How can you think that I'd care what people like Wyatt would say? How could you think that I'd care what anyone but you and I think?"

"But our lives are so different..." But even to her own ears, that sounded weak.

"Do you know why we were friends?" Oh, he looked so dangerous right now. "Because you treated me like any other kid. And I hope I did the same to you. You were never just the maid's daughter to me, babe. You were always Sofia. And I hope I was never just a rich boy to you. I..." He swallowed, looking suddenly nervous. "I was Eric to you. Wasn't I?"

"Of course you were—are," she sobbed. "But I can't ask this of you, Eric. My kids and I are not your responsibility."

"You're not asking—I am." He pressed a kiss to her forehead and despite everything, she felt it all the way down to her toes. "Aren't you listening? I never do anything I don't want to. I'm here with you, babe. I was here last week and I'll be here next week. You mean too much to me for one bad moment to make me walk away from you."

He was making too much sense. Way, way too much sense. There were objections, she knew there were. But darned if she could remember them right now. "But..."

"And I'm not trying to replace David," he said.

"He'll always be a part of you and he'll always be a part of the twins. But you didn't die with him, Sofia. And I believe, deep in my heart, that he wouldn't want you to face raising those children by yourself." Her mouth opened to reply, but he cut her off. "Nothing against your parents, babe. They love you and the twins and they're wonderful people. But they can't be a father to your children." His voice dropped and he took a step closer to her. "They can't be a husband to you."

"That was low," she choked out, losing the battle to her tears. She didn't want to cry because if she started, she wasn't sure she'd be able to stop. Because the infuriating man was right. David wouldn't have wanted Sofia to feel like she was completely alone right now.

He would have wanted her to smile again.

Eric pulled her into his arms and it was as if a weight was lifted off her chest. For the first time in days, she could breathe again. "Then quit making me fight dirty and just accept that I'm not going anywhere." He stroked her hair as he said it and damn it, she was comforted. "I missed you," he said into her hair. "You didn't come to work this week."

"I needed a few days," she admitted. "So much happened so quickly and I just…" She hadn't been able to deal with it.

"I know. And I made it worse, didn't I? I sprung the idea of the condo and living together on you and you…"

She choked out a little laugh. "And I felt horribly guilty. I still do."

That got him to lean back. "Guilty? Why?"

"My babies were sick and I wasn't there for them. I was with…" She swallowed hard. "I was with you."

He stared down at her in surprise. "But they were with your parents. It's not like you left them all alone."

She had no idea how she was even supposed to explain mommy guilt to him. "But I have to focus on them. I…I love you, too. But I have to put them first, don't you see?"

Hope flared in his eyes but it quickly turned into something fiercer. "So you're going to what—martyr yourself for them?"

"No, of course not." But even as she said it, she wondered if maybe there wasn't a little truth to that. "But they need me. They're only babies, Eric. I'm all they've got."

He took a step away from her and then spun to fix her with a glare. "Get in the car."

"What?"

"I have to tell you something and I'd rather not do it in public." He opened the car door and motioned. "In, Sofia."

Feeling nervous, she climbed in. He slid in after her and slammed the door. For a tense moment, they sat there. Then he pressed a button and said, "Drive."

Instantly, the car began to move. "Eric?"

"My fiancée was three months pregnant with another man's baby," he blurted out. "When she stood me up. We hadn't had sex in six months because she said it would make our wedding night more 'special' and you know what? I didn't fight for her. I let her slip away."

Sofia gasped and covered her mouth with her hand. "And the baby…"

"Paternity tests confirmed it—not mine. Do you want to know what's funny, Sofia? I don't miss Prudence at all. Not the sex, not the silence that always existed between us, not her. But when I found out about the baby…"

He stared out the window. "I was ready and willing to fight for that baby. But he wasn't mine and Prudence married his father less than two weeks after she left me."

"Eric, I had no idea."

"No one does, outside of Prudence's family and the private investigators. So far, I've kept it quiet."

She reached over and wrapped her fingers around his. "I'm sorry."

"I only tell you this now because I want you to understand—when I say I love your kids, I don't just mean in that generic, all-babies-are-cute kind of way." He took a deep breath and turned wet eyes in her direction. "I can buy anything, do anything I want."

"You mentioned a duck costume," she murmured.

"Anything," he repeated with more force. "Except I can't buy the love of a good woman and a family. I didn't mourn losing Prudence because she was never mine to lose. But I mourned that little boy. I had no idea how much I wanted to be a father until I thought I might be one. That was taken away from me, too. Then you showed up, an old friend who was much too easy to love, with a pair of toddlers who needed a father and…"

He blinked hard and Sofia's eyes watered. "I'm not trying to replace David, Sofia. But you're more than I'd ever thought I'd find because I don't just love you. You're my friend. You're my everything."

Oh, hell. How was she supposed to argue with that? "You've given me a reason to smile again," she told him through her tears. "I didn't know I could still smile for myself. But I didn't want you to think that the only reason I took the job or the clothes or the weekend together was because I was trying to snag you. I didn't want you to think I was like that."

He laughed. "The more things change, Sofia, the more they stay the same and you were never like that. You've always fit with me. It never mattered who you were when we were kids—you were just my friend. It's the same now, except that I love you. None of the other stuff matters except for this." He took both of her hands in his. "Marry me, babe. Let me be your family. And when you stumble, let me be there to make sure you don't fall again."

"You're sure it can work?" But even as she asked the question, she knew she was being ridiculous.

"I'm Eric Jenner," he reminded her, as if she could

forget. "I can make anything work. Even twin toddlers."

She laughed and threw her arms around him. "Yes. You make me happy. You make me smile," she told him. And she'd missed smiling.

"Babe, I'm going to make you smile every day for the rest of our lives."

"Promise?"

He lowered his mouth to hers. "Oh, yeah—that's a promise I'm looking forward to keeping."

Epilogue

"On three," Eric said, treading water. The lake was cool and crisp—which, given that the temperature was close to one hundred, was a welcome relief.

"One," Eddy Jenner said in a very serious tone. Eric couldn't fight the smile as he held up his fingers to count off. "Two…three!" And then the boy launched himself into the air.

Eric hurriedly paddled backward, barely getting his arms up in time to catch Eddy before they both plunged under the surface of the lake. When they resurfaced seconds later, Eddy was squealing with delight and Eric was laughing.

"My turn, Daddy—my turn!" Addy insisted, stamping her little foot on the deck of his boat. Both of the kids wore wet suits with built-in floaties and what wasn't covered by fabric was slathered with the highest SPF known to womankind.

Sofia insisted and who was Eric to say no to his wife? Besides, it was no hardship to have her rub sunscreen all over his back. And chest. And arms. Lord knew he enjoyed returning the favor. Sun protection was *sexy*.

Eric pushed Eddy back toward the boat and swam alongside him to make sure that the three-year-old wasn't struggling, but he didn't need to worry. The kids took to water like ducks. When they were in the pool at his parents' house, Eric didn't even put them in floaties. He just made sure they stayed in the shallow end, where he could get to them at all times.

Sofia was waiting for Eddy by the ladder. "You're going to be doing this all day long, you know that?" she asked Eric with that smile he loved.

"If you want a turn, I'll catch you, babe," he said, waggling his eyebrows at her.

She laughed and then leaned forward suggestively, her breasts practically spilling out of the bikini top. "You can catch me later."

Eric flopped back in the water, pretending to faint. She killed him every single day. It was a crime, how good his wife looked in that bikini. Especially now that she was four months pregnant. While she always looked good in a bikini—red, forever red—the way her body had changed so far was nothing short of a revelation. And it went far beyond her stunning breasts. He found the gentle swell of her stomach to be unbelievably erotic. After a rough three months, Sofia had promised him that the second trimester was the fun one and they were just getting started.

She was a wonder, his Sofia.

"Daddy!" Addy said, scolding his lack of attention. Sofia winked at him as Addy said, "Catch me!"

"Count to three," he told his daughter.

She pushed her hair out of her face and counted very solemnly before screaming her way out onto the water. Eric caught her and they laughed as they bobbed together.

As he helped Addy back to the ladder, Eric looked up at his wife and smiled again. This was his life now. He loved his wife. What he and Sofia had was a bright, passionate love that got stronger over time, not weaker. It was no joke to say that she was his best friend and every day, he worked hard making sure he was her best friend, too.

In another hour, the twins would be worn out from all of this jumping. He and Sofia would put them down for a nap in their room in the yacht and then he and his wife would steal half an hour to themselves in their own cabin. Warm from the sun and relaxed by the water, Eric was never happier than when he was making love to his wife on this boat. Then, she would rest while he piloted them back to the pier. Tonight, they'd have dinner at his parents' house. Sofia's parents were coming, too—one big happy family.

Finally, he had everything he wanted. And the

more things changed—the twins growing up, the new baby, maybe a bigger boat—the more they would stay the same.

Sofia had his heart and he had hers.

He'd earned the one thing money couldn't buy.

* * * * *

If you liked this story of passion and family
from Sarah M. Anderson,
pick up these other titles!

NOT THE BOSS'S BABY
HIS LOST AND FOUND FAMILY
THE NANNY PLAN
HIS SON, HER SECRET

Available now from Harlequin Desire!

***

And don't miss the next
BILLIONAIRES AND BABIES *story,*
THE CHRISTMAS BABY BONUS,
by USA TODAY *bestselling author*
Yvonne Lindsay.

Available December 2017!
If you're on Twitter, tell us what you think
of Harlequin Desire! #harlequindesire

*Can a former bad boy and the woman
he never forgot find true love during one
unforgettable Christmas?
Find out in CHRISTMASTIME COWBOY,
the sizzling new* COPPER RIDGE *novel from*
New York Times *bestselling author Maisey Yates.
Read on for your sneak peek...*

LIAM DONNELLY WAS nobody's favorite.

Though being a favorite in their household growing up would never have meant much, Liam was confident that as much as both of his parents disdained their younger son, Alex, they hated Liam more.

And as much as his brothers loved him—or whatever you wanted to call their brand of affection—Liam knew he wasn't the one they'd carry out if there was a house fire. That was fine too.

It wasn't self-pity. It was just a fact.

But while he wasn't anyone's particular favorite, he knew he was at least one person's least favorite.

Sabrina Leighton hated him with every ounce of her beautiful, petite being. Not that he blamed her. But, considering they were having a business meeting today, he did hope that she could keep some of the hatred bottled up.

Liam got out of his truck and put his cowboy hat

on, surveying his surroundings. The winery spread was beautiful, with a large, picturesque house overlooking the grounds. The winery and the road leading up to it were carved into an Oregon mountainside. Trees and forest surrounded the facility on three sides, creating a secluded feeling. Like the winery was part of another world. In front of the first renovated barn was a sprawling lawn and a path that led down to the river. There was a seating area there and Liam knew that during the warmer months it was a nice place to hang out. Right now, it was too damned cold, and the damp air that blew up from the rushing water sent a chill straight through him.

He shoved his hands in his pockets and kept on walking. There were three rustic barns on the property that they used for weddings and dinners, and one that had been fully remodeled into a dining and tasting room.

He had seen the new additions online. He hadn't actually been to Grassroots Winery in the past thirteen years. That was part of the deal. The deal that had been struck back when Jamison Leighton was still owner of the place.

Back when Liam had been nothing more than a good-for-nothing, low-class troublemaker with a couple of misdemeanors to his credit.

Times changed.

Liam might still be all those things at heart, but he was also a successful businessman. And Jamison Leighton no longer owned Grassroots.

Some things, however, hadn't changed. The presence of Sabrina Leighton being one of them.

It had been thirteen years. But he couldn't pretend he thought everything was all right and forgiven. Not considering the way she had reacted when she had seen him at Ace's bar the past few months.

Small towns. Like everybody was at the same party and could only avoid each other for so long.

If it wasn't at the bar, they would most certainly end up at a four-way stop at the same time, or in the same aisle at the grocery store.

But today's meeting would not be accidental. Today's meeting was planned. He wondered if something would get thrown at him. It certainly wouldn't be the first time.

He walked across the gravel lot and into the dining room. It was empty, since the facility—a rustic barn with a wooden chandelier hanging in the center—had yet to open for the day. There was a bar with stools positioned at the front, and tables set up around the room. Back when he had worked here, there had been one basic tasting room, and nowhere for anyone to sit. Most of the wine had been sent out to retail stores for sale, rather than making the winery itself some kind of destination.

He wondered when all of that had changed. He imagined it had something to do with Lindy, the new owner and ex-wife of Jamison Leighton's son, Damien. As far as Liam knew, and he knew enough—considering he didn't get involved with business ventures without figuring out what he was getting into—Damien had drafted the world's dumbest prenuptial agreement. At least, it was dumb for a man who clearly had problems keeping his dick in his pants.

Though why Sabrina was still working at the winery when her sister-in-law had current ownership, and her brother had been deposed, and her parents were—from what he had read in public records—apoplectic about the loss of their family legacy, he didn't know. But he assumed he would find out. At about the same time he found out whether or not something was going to get thrown at his head.

The door from the back opened, and he gritted his teeth. Because, no matter how prepared he felt philosophically to see Sabrina, he knew that there would be impact. There always was. A damned funny thing, that one woman could live in the back of his mind the way she had for so long. That no matter how many years or how many women he put between them, she still burned bright and hot in his memory.

That no matter that he had steeled himself to run into her—because he knew how small towns worked—the impact was like a brick to the side of his head every single time.

She appeared a moment after the door opened, looking severe. Overly so. Her blond hair was pulled back into a high ponytail, and she was wearing a black sheath dress that went down past her knees but conformed to curves that were more generous than they'd been thirteen years ago.

In a good way.

"Hello, Liam," she said, her tone impersonal. Had she not used his first name, it might have been easy to pretend that she didn't know who he was.

"Sabrina."

"Lindy told me that you wanted to talk about a potential joint venture. And since that falls under my jurisdiction as manager of the tasting room, she thought we might want to work together."

Now she was smiling.

The smile was so brittle it looked like it might crack her face.

"Yes, I'm familiar with the details. Particularly since this venture was my idea." He let a small silence hang there for a beat before continuing. "I'm looking at an empty building on the end of Main Street. It would be more than just a tasting room. It would be a small café with some retail space."

"How would it differ from Lane Donnelly's store? She already offers specialty foods."

"Well, we would focus on Grassroots wine and Laughing Irish cheese. Also, I would happily purchase products from Lane's to give the menu a local focus. The café would be nothing big. Just a small lunch place with wine. Very limited selection. Very specialty. But I feel like in a tourist location, that's what you want."

"Great," she said, her smile remaining completely immobile.

He took that moment to examine her more closely. The changes in her face over the years. She was more beautiful now than she had been at seventeen. Her slightly round, soft face had refined in the ensuing years, her cheekbones now more prominent, the angle of her chin sharper.

Her eyebrows looked different too. When she'd been a teenager, they'd been thinner, rounder. Now they were a bit stronger, more angular.

"Great," he returned. "I guess we can go down and have a look at the space sometime this week. Gage West is the owner of the property, and he hasn't listed it yet. Handily, my sister-in-law is good friends with his wife. Both of my sisters-in-law, actually. So I got the inside track on that."

Her expression turned bland. "How impressive."

She sounded absolutely unimpressed. "It wasn't intended to be impressive. Just useful."

She sighed slowly. "Did you have a day of the week in mind to go view the property? Because I really am very busy."

"Are you?"

"Yes," she responded, that smile spreading over her face again. "This is a very demanding job, plus I do have a life."

She stopped short of saying exactly what that life entailed.

"Too busy to do this, which is part of your actual job?" he asked.

On the surface she looked calm, but he could sense a dark energy beneath that spoke of a need to savage him. "I had my schedule sorted out for the next couple of weeks. This is coming together more quickly than expected."

"I'll work something out with Gage and give Lindy a call, how about that?"

"You don't have to call Lindy. I'll give you my phone number. You can call or text me directly."

She reached over to the counter and took a card from the rustic surface, extending her hand toward him. He reached out and took the card, their fingertips brushing as they made the handoff.

And he felt it. Straight down to his groin, where he had always felt things for her, even though it was impossible. Even though he was all wrong for her. And even though now they were doing a business deal together, and she looked like she would cheerfully chew through his flesh if given half the chance.

She might be smiling, but he didn't trust that smile. He was still waiting. Waiting for her to shout recriminations at him now that they were alone. Every other time he had encountered her over the past four months it had been in public. Twice in Ace's bar, and once walking down the street, where she had made a very quick sharp left to avoid walking past him.

It had not been subtle, and it had certainly not spoken of somebody who was over the past.

So his assumption had been that if the two of them were ever alone she was going to let him have it. But she didn't. Instead, she gave him that card and then began to look...bored.

"Did you need anything else?" she asked.

"Not really. Though I have some spreadsheet information that you might want to look over. Ideas that I have for the layout, the menu. It is getting a little ahead of ourselves, in case we end up not liking the venue."

"You've been to look at the venue already, haven't you?" It was vaguely accusatory.

"I have been there, yes. But again, I believe in preparedness. I was hardly going to get very deep into this if I didn't think it was viable. Personally, I'm interested in making sure that we have diverse interests. The economy doesn't typically favor farms, Sabrina. And that is essentially what my brothers and I have. I expect an uphill fight to make that place successful."

She tilted her head to the side. "Like you said, you do your research."

Her friendliness was beginning to slip. And he waited. For something else. For something to get thrown at him. It didn't happen.

"That I do. Take these," he said, handing her the folder that he was holding on to. He made sure their fingers didn't touch this time. "And we'll talk next week."

Then he turned and walked away from her, and he resisted the strong impulse to turn back and get one more glance at her. It wasn't the first time he had resisted that.

He had a feeling it wouldn't be the last.

As soon as Liam walked out of the tasting room, Sabrina let out a breath that had been killing her to keep in. A breath that contained about a thousand insults and recriminations. And more than a few very colorful swear word combinations. A breath that nearly burned her throat, because it was full of so many sharp and terrible things.

She lifted her hands to her face and realized they were shaking. It had been thirteen years. Why did he still affect her like this? Maybe, just maybe, if she had ever found a man who made her feel even half of what Liam did, she wouldn't have such a hard time dealing with him. The feelings wouldn't be so strong.

But she hadn't. So that supposition was basically moot.

The worst part was the tattoos. He'd had about three when he'd been nineteen. Now they covered both of his arms, and she had the strongest urge to make them as familiar to her as the original tattoos had been. To memorize each and every detail about them.

The tree was the one that really caught her attention. The Celtic knots, she knew, were likely a nod to his Irish heritage, but the tree—whose branches she could see stretching down from his shoulder—she was curious about what that meant.

"And you are spending too much time thinking about him," she admonished herself.

She shouldn't be thinking about him at all. She should just focus on congratulating herself for saying nothing stupid. At least she hadn't cried and demanded answers for the night he had completely laid waste to her every feeling.

"How did it go?"

Sabrina turned and saw her sister-in-law, Lindy, come in. People would be forgiven for thinking that she and Lindy were actually biological sisters. In fact, they looked much more alike than Sabrina and her younger sister Beatrix did.

Like Sabrina, Lindy had long, straight blond hair. Bea, on the other hand, had freckles all over her face and a wild riot of reddish-brown curls that resisted taming almost as strongly as the youngest Leighton sibling herself did.

That was another thing Sabrina and Lindy had in common. They were predominantly tame. At least, they kept things as together as they possibly could on the surface.

"Fine."

"You didn't savage him with a cheese knife?"

"Lindy," Sabrina said, "please. This is dry-clean

only." She waved her hand up and down, indicating her dress.

"I don't know what your whole issue is with him..."

Because no one spoke of it. Lindy had married Sabrina's brother after the unpleasantness. It was no secret that Sabrina and her father were estranged—even if it was a brittle, quiet estrangement. But unless Damien had told Lindy the details—and Sabrina doubted he knew all of them—her sister-in-law wouldn't know the whole story.

"I don't have an issue with him," Sabrina said. "I knew him thirteen years ago. That has nothing to do with now. It has nothing to do with this new venture for the winery. Which I am on board with one hundred percent." It was true. She was.

"Well," Lindy said, "that's good to hear."

She could tell that Lindy didn't believe her. "It's going to be fine. I'm looking forward to this." That was also true. Mostly. She was looking forward to expanding Grassroots. Looking forward to helping build the winery, and making it into something that was truly theirs. So that her parents could no longer shout recriminations about Lindy stealing something from the Leighton family.

Eventually, they would make the winery so much more successful that most of it would be theirs.

And if her own issues with her parents were tangled up in all of this, then...that was just how it was.

Sabrina wanted it all to work, and work well. If for

no other reason than to prove to Liam Donnelly that she was no longer the seventeen-year-old girl whose world he'd wrecked all those years ago.

In some ways, Sabrina envied the tangible ways in which Lindy had been able to exact revenge on Damien. Of course, Sabrina's relationship with Liam wasn't anything like a ten-year marriage ended by infidelity. She gritted her teeth. She did her best not to think about Liam. About the past. Because it hurt. Every damn time it hurt. It didn't matter if it should or not.

But now that he was back in Copper Ridge, now that she sometimes just happened to run into him, it was worse. It was harder not to think about him.

Him and the grand disaster that had happened after.

* * * * *

Look for CHRISTMASTIME COWBOY, available from Maisey Yates and HQN Books wherever books are sold.

COMING NEXT MONTH FROM

HARLEQUIN

Desire

Available December 5, 2017

#2557 HIS SECRET SON
The Westmoreland Legacy • by Brenda Jackson
The SEAL who fathered Bristol's son died a hero's death...or so she
was told. But now Coop is back and vowing to claim his child! Her
son deserves to know his father, so Bristol must find a way to fight
temptation...and keep her heart safe.

#2558 BEST MAN UNDER THE MISTLETOE
Texas Cattleman's Club: Blackmail • by Jules Bennett
Planning a wedding with the gorgeous, sexy best man would have been a
lot easier if he weren't Chelsea Hunt's second-worst enemy. Gabe Walsh
is furious that the sins of his uncle have also fallen on him, but soon his
desire to prove his innocence turns into the desire to make her his!

#2559 THE CHRISTMAS BABY BONUS
Billionaires and Babies • by Yvonne Lindsay
Getting snowed in with his sexy assistant is difficult enough. But when
an abandoned baby is found in the stables, die-hard bachelor Piers may
find himself yearning for a family for Christmas...

#2560 LITTLE SECRETS: HIS PREGNANT SECRETARY
Little Secrets • by Joanne Rock
After a heated argument with his secretary turns sexually explosive,
entrepreneur Jager McNeill knows the right thing to do is propose...
because now she's carrying his child! But what will he do when she
won't settle for a marriage of convenience?

#2561 SNOWED IN WITH A BILLIONAIRE
Secrets of the A-List • by Karen Booth
Joy McKinley just *had* to be rescued by one of the wealthiest, sexiest
men she's ever met. Especially when she's hiding out in someone
else's house under a name that isn't hers. But when they get snowed in
together, can their romance survive the truth?

#2562 BABY IN THE MAKING
Accidental Heirs • by Elizabeth Bevarly
Surprise heir Hannah Robinson will lose her fortune if she doesn't get
pregnant. Enter daredevil entrepreneur Yeager Novak...and the child
they'll make together! Opposites attract on this baby-making adventure,
but will that be enough to turn their pact into a real romance?

YOU CAN FIND MORE INFORMATION ON UPCOMING HARLEQUIN® TITLES,
FREE EXCERPTS AND MORE AT WWW.HARLEQUIN.COM.

HDCNM1117

Get 2 Free Books,
Plus 2 Free Gifts—
just for trying the Reader Service!

Laramie stared at Bristol. "You were pregnant?"

"Yes," she said in a soft voice. "And you're free to order a
paternity test if you need to verify that my son is yours."

He had a son? It took less than a second for his emotions to
go from shock to disbelief. "How?"

She lifted a brow. "Probably from making love almost
nonstop for three solid days."

They had definitely done that. Although he'd used a condom
each and every time, he knew there was always a possibility
that something could go wrong.

"And where is he?" he asked.

"At home."

Where the hell was that? It bothered him how little he knew about the woman who'd just announced she'd given birth to his child. At least she'd tried contacting him to let him know. Some women would not have done so.

If his child had been born nine months after their holiday fling, that meant he would have turned two in September. While Laramie was in a cell, somewhere in the world, Bristol had been giving life.

To his child.

Emotions Laramie had never felt before suddenly bombarded him with the impact of a Tomahawk missile. He was a parent, which meant he had to think about someone other than himself. He wasn't sure how he felt about that. But then, wasn't he used to taking care of others as a member of his SEAL team?

She nodded. "I'm not asking you for anything Laramie, if that's what you're thinking. I just felt you had a right to know about the baby."

She wasn't asking him for anything? Did she not know her bold declaration that he'd fathered her child demanded everything?

"I want to see him."

"You will. I would never keep Laramie from you."

"You named him Laramie?" Even more emotions swamped him. Her son—their son—had his name?

She hesitated. "Yes."

Then he asked, "So, what's your reason for giving yourself my last name, as well?"

Don't miss
HIS SECRET SON
by New York Times *bestselling author Brenda Jackson,*
available December 2017
wherever Harlequin® Desire books and ebooks are sold.

www.Harlequin.com

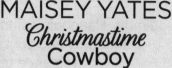

LOVE
Harlequin
romance?

Join our Harlequin community to share your thoughts and connect with other romance readers!

Be the first to find out about promotions, news, and exclusive content!

Sign up for the Harlequin e-newsletter and download a free book from any series at

www.TryHarlequin.com

Want to give in to temptation with
steamy tales of irresistible desire?

Check out **Harlequin® Presents®,
Harlequin® Desire** and
Harlequin® Kimani™ Romance books!

New books available every month!

CONNECT WITH US AT:

Harlequin.com/Community

ReaderService.com

**ROMANCE WHEN
YOU NEED IT**

PGENRE2017

HARLEQUIN®

A *Romance* FOR EVERY MOOD™

Love the Harlequin book you just read?

Your opinion matters.

Review this book on your favorite book site, review site, blog or your own social media properties and share your opinion with other readers!